KEY WEST
BONEYARD
MIKE PETTIT

Key West Boneyard

A Jack Marsh Action Thriller

Mike Pettit

Edited by CDC Editing Services.

Cover by VooDoo Graphics

4

Dedication

Robert D. Pettit

Thomas B. Pettit

No Greater Love

KEY WEST BONEYARD

JACK MARSH ACTION MYSTERY

A blanket of humidity hung over Key West like a gloved hand squeezing a soft throat, holding in the smell of mold and dry rot from the hundreds of old homes and buildings which had been built and rebuilt over the same ground for several hundred years. New structures, continually, replaced the old, as decay and time did their job. Worm-eaten keels circled the island, their rotted ribs reaching skyward, like bony fingers from a watery grave, as a testament to nature's power. The relentless sun and deadly storms added to the carnage heaped upon the island, ravaging and destroying what mortal men tried to build, in a never-ending cycle. The island had always been a place of hopes and dreams, of fortunes made and lost, of living and dying. From a celestial vantage point, however, the island looked more like a graveyard than a tropical paradise.

The stink of rotted tropical vegetation, dead fish, seaweed, and human waste, mixed with the sweet smells of jasmine, bougainvillea, and banana, of tanning oils and whiskey, catalytic converters and fossil fuels, all combining to make Key West pass for a modern day tropical paradise. The only difference between Key West's brand of paradise and Montego Bay in Jamaica was that Key West had a road in and out, giving the locals a way to escape, if life got too hard. Ask any local, and he will tell you, *"When ting's get bod in*

Montego, mon, you fucked. Dat be dat, Brada. But, Key West, she be sweet. Mon sticks his tumb out and he go up-island like da wind."

Jack Marsh sat at the bar sipping his third whiskey of the afternoon, eyeing the two dozen or so customers scattered around the Sand Bar's interior. Jack had a buzz on and wasn't feeling any pain. The familiar sounds and smells of the bar were like a security blanket that protected him from the storm building off to the east. Distant thunder was starting to compete with the Sand Bar's entertainer, Johnny Boofey, as he sang a loud and drunken rendition of Joe Cocker's *Cry Me a River* up on the stage. His partner, Monica (no last name), accompanied him in a breast-jiggling doo-wop rhythm in her skimpy costume that kept the male customers drinking and ogling. Johnny Boofey was one of those gifted singers who could imitate just about every other singer in the business, and did six nights a week, with one day off to sober up. The unusual thing about Johnny was that he couldn't sing worth a damn in his own voice, but give him the name of any song sung in the last fifty years, and by God, the man could wail. In addition to a generous financial contract, Johnny insisted that he have a quart of Jack Daniels waiting for him on stage each night, and if he was having a good night, a second bottle would be sent up to him. Almost every night, Monica would pour Johnny into a cab and the two would disappear into Key West's underbelly, only to show up the next evening clean, shaved, sober, and ready to sing.

Jack dug an ice cube out of his glass and plopped it into his mouth, enjoying the chill on his throat as it melted. It had been miserably hot all afternoon, with not a breath of air moving, as the town prepared for hurricane number three to move in. The locals, with any sense, had started their storm preparation early, putting up shutters and paneling, stocking up on basics like water and booze. Those residents, without common sense, continued their daily routine of plotting ways to scam the tourists and visitors out of a few bucks.

Jack had heard that the hottest new scam working Duval Street was the Snake Lady, decked out in a genie outfit with heavy mascara around her painted face and scarves hiding her midriff stretch marks. For five bucks, she would drape her twelve-foot python around a brave tourist's neck and then snap a photo for the terrified soul to share back home. What the tourists did not know was that the Snake Lady shot-up her snake every morning with enough Novocain to fast freeze a…well, a python, rendering him harmless for the few hours she worked the streets. Rumors floating down the back alleys were that the chicken population around the airport had thinned out considerably since the Snake Lady had arrived in town. Jack laughed, when he heard about the reward being offered by the sheriff for information leading to an arrest. Several of the more ingenious alley dwellers had taken to following the Snake Lady around, waiting for the snake to have a bowel movement, so they could move in to inspect the scat for signs of chicken bones, feet, or maybe even a case-breaking beak. So far, luck had eluded them. There was even talk that the Snake Lady had been chased out of Key Largo when a small child went missing. After all, she was an Eastern European with an accent, possibly even gypsy, or any one of those eastern bloc countries.

The Sand Bar, on the corner of Duval and Eaton Streets, never closed. As long as a paying customer was able to order and pay for a drink, Jack kept the place open. The Sand Bar was one of the larger and more popular watering holes on Duval. It was known for its generous sized drinks, greasy burgers, and fish sandwiches, but, most of all, for the good-looking servers, dressed in skimpy halter-tops and shorts, who served the ice-cold drinks and flirted with the customers. Jack vowed he would never leave Key West…even if he could. The Keys were the end of the line for him. Key West was his last refuge before having to skip the country and head for the Caribbean Islands.

After five years of island life, he was beginning to think that his ex-wife and her deceased father's attorneys had given up looking for him. There were rumblings about a mutual fund scam gone bad that his father-in-law was behind, and his ex-wife thought that Jack knew more about it than was ever made known by her father. The day the old man had a sudden heart attack and died, Jack skimmed a half-million dollars out of the fund's secret account and disappeared into the wind. At the time, he felt it was a fair payback for all the crap he had taken off the old man. He had covered for him, on several occasions, with lies and cooking the firm's books. In hindsight, he wished that he had taken all the money in the account. After all, it was on his advice and knowhow that the old man grew the fund.

Because of the old man's greed and hunger for control, he had insisted that everything within the firm was in his name only. Jack was on the company books as a junior account manager, within the firm, but with no authority. His only claim to any notoriety was that he was married to the boss's promiscuous daughter, who had slept with every man in L.A., and he was laughed at, behind his back. With the old man's death, there was nothing to trace any criminal wrongdoing back to Jack, so, he cleared out his desk, his joint personal account with his wife, their safety deposit box with all her jewels, and his framed MBA diploma from Cal State, and split.

The wind blew him down to Key West where he hooked up with a Marine buddy in a salvage and dive business. With the money that was left over, he bought the Sand Bar, paid cash, signed the papers, and moved into the upstairs apartment over the bar. That night, the old owner caught the last flight out and had not been heard from since. Rumor had him spotted in Rio, Bogotá, and, as far away as Bangkok, but nothing about what he was running from. Five years later, the Sand Bar was a gold mine and a hugely popular party-stop for tourists and a watering hole for locals. Jack's big money, however, came in from various salvage jobs and several off-the-wall adventures that ran a thin line between being illegal and downright criminal. It was never Jack's intention to get involved in questionable activities, or do anything that would draw attention to him. His objective was to lay low and out of sight. Opportunities just seemed to fall on him. Maybe because he was known as a stand-up guy that would help a friend in trouble, or maybe it was just the way things went down in Key West. Whatever the cause, Jack had a reputation of being a man not to fuck with, but also a man you could go to if you were in something over your head.

Jack's years of running the streets of L.A., as a tough kid with a druggie mother and an alcoholic father, taught him early how to spot trouble and face it head-on. By the time he was seventeen, there were not many illegal things he hadn't done, and was told by a juvenile judge to join the Marines or go to juvvie. Jack had his mother sign the release papers, and the next day, he was gone. His years on the street prepared him for his tour with the Marine Corps. It proved to be a perfect matchup. From the first day in boot camp, he loved the mental and physical challenge, the camaraderie. The Corps became the home he never had. He thrived on the discipline and regimentation and he pushed himself to excel in every aspect of his new world. Jack was a natural born leader and, soon, found himself in Iraq, fighting Hussein's elite Republican Guard. After returning to the U.S., his plan was to go to college and get a degree, then rejoin the Corps as an officer and be a twenty-year man. Jack applied for admission to college and was accepted at Cal Poly, where he received a B.S. and a Masters in economics, and met his wife to be. One thing led to another, time went by, and he married into the good life of wealth and privilege. He was soon disgusted with his life. He was trapped working for his father-in-law, and felt betrayed by his wife's infidelity. He began to drink heavily, and started looking for a way out. When it came, he did not waste a second dusting L.A. off his heels.

Chapter 2

As the afternoon sweltered on, Jack sat at the bar sipping chilled whiskey and crunching ice as he watched two of his more vocal employees wrestle with the storm shutters. He couldn't shake the feeling of foreboding, of something waiting, something out there in the bushes. Experience had taught him to not ignore these feelings. Jack got off his barstool and went out to the sidewalk, sniffed the still air, and looked up and down Duval for anything out of place. He took his time and scanned the rooflines, peered into faces, watched the traffic pattern, things he had learned to do in Fallujah. When trouble comes, it can be from any angle. Nothing out of the ordinary pushed his alarm buttons, but he was still uneasy. Trouble was coming, he just didn't know from what direction.

Lamont and Little Junior were struggling with a four by eight sheet of plywood in front of the Sand Bar, as the first gusts of wind blew into town. A strong gusty shear whistled by and Lamont lost his grip of his end. Little Junior yelped loudly, went airborne, and sailed across Eaton Street, hanging onto the sheet of wood before crashing into the curb.

"Lamont, you muthafucka! You trying to get me killed?" Junior screamed.

Lamont Jackson limped across the street to help the younger man up. "I couldn't hold on, J. This cast won't let me move my foot without twisting me around. I had to let go."

"Yeah, seems to me that foot gets you out of an awful lot of work around here. Seems to me that broken ankle should be healed by now, so you can stop giving me all the crap jobs and maybe cut me some slack."

"Hold on right there, my little Brother. I am the boss, you are the employee. If I say you do, then you do. If I say you don't, you don't. If I say my foot hurts, then that is the end of that. You with me on this?"

"You ain't the boss. Ms. Coco's the boss. If I tell her you just shining everybody on she's going to believe me..."

"Believe you? Why is she going to believe you? You ain't nothing but a skinny ass..."

"She's going to believe me, because she's in love with me..."

"*Say What*! She's in love with you?"

"Who's in love with whom?" Jack said, as he stepped out of the bar to see what all the fuss was about.

"Jack, this child says Ms. Coco's in love with him and that he could just say a few words and get me fired, if I didn't start helping out more around here," Lamont said, as he threw his upper body into his limp, exaggerating the movement with a painful grimace plastered across his face.

Jack stopped in midstride and with a skeptical look said, "Did Ms. Coco tell you that she was in love with you, Junior?"

"Well, not exactly in words, but I can tell these things, Mr. Marsh. Women are easy to read. You just have to look for the signs. You know what I'm saying?"

"Uh, no, I don't think I do, Junior. Give me a couple of examples. Maybe, I can use some of your moves on a couple of ladies I have my eye on," Jack said, conspiratorially.

"Well, Mr. Marsh, you being a white dude and all it may not work for you, but I'll try," Junior said, lowering his eyelids to half-mast and puckered his lips rapidly three or four times.

"You see that? That's the one that get you more lovin' than any other thing I know," Junior said, proudly.

Jack and Lamont looked at each other in disbelief and burst out laughing. "Did you do that to Ms. Coco?" Jack asked.

"Well, not yet, but I'm going to tonight. She's ready for me to make my move."

"Junior, listen to me. If you value your life, you do not want to do that to Ms. Coco. I don't think she would appreciate the implied meaning of your gesture, or that it's coming from a teenaged wannabe gangbanger."

"Mr. Marsh, those are some hard words. You don't understand, I'm in love with that woman. I got it all figured out, I'm going to work hard and someday I'll have Lamont's job and have plenty of money…"

"My job! You are not getting my job! What the fuck you talking about? Besides, school starts back up in three weeks and you will be there sitting in the front row when they open. I do not want to hear any more about loving or secret moves. You are going to finish school and then go to college. Ain't no other way, boy."

"*Boy*! *Who you calling boy*!" Junior jumped up and hit Lamont in the chin.

Lamont's chin was harder than rolled steel and he just laughed it off.

"You don't want me to break a foot off up your ass, Junior. Now, let's get these storm shutters up before the rain starts," he said, smacking Junior on the butt and bent to lift the plywood.

Chapter 3

Flashes of lightning screamed across the rooftops, like crazed banshees snapping at anything that stood in their way. Behind the megaton flashes came a rolling blitzkrieg of thunder, with a deafening nonstop barrage of explosions that drowned out all other sounds. A steady forty-knot wind skittered newspapers and trash down streets and alleys, and around partiers, as they happily drank their way up and down Duval Street, oblivious to the approaching storm. The visitors were here to party, and by God, a measly Cat-2 Hurricane named Misty was not going to slow them down.

Even with the approaching storm, business was good. As soon as the rain blew in, the place filled up and the action kicked in. Jack eased off his "owners stool" and started down the backside of the bar, stopping long enough to top off his glass with crushed ice and pour himself another drink, quickly slurping at the edges as it overflowed.

"Don't you think you should slow down on the hard stuff, Jack?" Coco Duvalier asked, busily preparing three drinks at the ready-station.

"Back off, woman. I'm just relaxing a little, and don't need any lecture on the evils of drinking," Jack slurred. "Besides, I have a lot on my mind."

Coco wiped her hands and stood close to Jack, "Jack, you need to forget about all that stuff that happened out on South Turk. It's over. Everyone is safe, Lamont is on the mend, the investigation is closed, and you were cleared of any criminal wrongdoing," she said, rubbing his shoulder muscles. "The women you saved are back with their families and are being cared for. Wasn't that your goal, to save those poor women?"

"Yeah, part of it. It just seems that at some point it got out of hand and the next thing I knew, I was enjoying the hell out of the things we were doing. Bill Price said the final tally on the dead and wounded in that fiasco was fourteen dead, four missing, and three WIA. All because I was nosey and opened that shipping container..."

"Jack, that's not fair to you. You didn't kill all those men. According to Bill, the Israelis were pulling out of the human trafficking and drug business anyway. There still would have been all those killings with or without you involved."

"Yeah, well, my greed started the ball rolling. I just can't get the whole mess out of my mind, Coco. Maybe I should take a vacation, get away from the Keys for a while. I came here to slow down, to get my life back on track, not to be constantly walking into things that aren't any of my business," he said, as he moved back to his stool and plopped down.

Chapter 4

Coco Duvalier busily wiped the bar top and stacked clean glasses on the back mirrored wall, continuing to worry about Jack's drinking. It wasn't like him to be so down. Maybe, he needed something else to come along, to pull him out of his funk. Meanwhile, she would keep an eye on him. She caught sight of herself in the bar's mirror and smiled back at the tall, well-built, light-skinned woman staring back at her. In fact, her aunt, because of her cocoa color, named her Coco. Her real name was Simone Duvalier. Coco's life had changed so much from when she stepped into the Sand Bar to get out of the heavy rainstorm three years ago. She had been hustling on Duval Street with a few other girls from Miami's Little Haiti when the rain started to pour. Rather than get soaked, she took refuge inside a bar to wait it out, then try for a couple of more tricks before the night was over. The bar was packed with visitors and tourists down for a big four-day weekend. Jack spotted her for what she was, a working girl trying to make a living. The storm increased and he allowed her to sleep in the kitchen overnight, if she wanted, but cautioned her to stay away from his customers. The next morning, she woke early and began to clean the place, as a show of appreciation. Since that day, the only time she missed work was to visit her aunt and uncle in Little Haiti once a month. Coco worked hard, gaining Jack's trust and friendship. She was now the bar's manager and handled all it's affairs, with Jack's total trust.

Coco ran her eyes over the drinking crowd huddled inside of the Sand Bar, out of the wind and approaching storm. The drinkers were enjoying the music, throwing down drinks, tossing bits of food at Armando, the resident foul-mouthed parrot who had come with the place when Jack bought it. For the first six months, Jack tried every trick he could think of to get rid of the bird, but nothing worked. He finally gave up after the night he drove the bird up to Marathon and put it inside a car parked in front of the Wooden Spoon Café. When Jack arrived back at the Sand Bar, Armando was on his perch, drunk as a sailor, and singing, *Yo Ho Ho, You Dirty, Son of a Bitch*. After that, Jack gave up and left him alone. Armando was now considered an important part of the Sand Bar and its reputation as a fun place to party while in Key West. He knew several dozen words, all dirty. His favorite was to call out, *"Show Me Your Tits, Show Me Your Tits,"* to all the women patrons. If a woman was drunk enough to flash Armando, he would respond with, *"Pancakes, Pancakes, serve 'em Up,"* or, *"Put 'em away, Put 'em away...Pleeeze,"* and then duck screech, as he was bombarded with french-fries and catcalls.

Coco's eyes stopped roving, when she spied a man standing in the shadows just inside the Eaton Street entrance. There was something familiar about him but she couldn't put her finger on it. A bolt of lightning shot across the sky making the bar lights flicker off and on for several moments but they stayed on. The man was gone. A chill ran down her back, when he suddenly reappeared in the shadows on the other side of the wide opening. She sucked in her breath, as the man pointed a finger at her and motioned for her to come to him. She could see the whites of his eyes as he stared at her and continued to motion for her to come. She wanted to ignore the man, but something about him held her attention. She was curious and afraid at the same time, so without a word, she started over to him.

"Mademoiselle Duvalier, you are to come with me. There is someone who wishes to speak with you. Come, quietly, as he won't be denied."

"What are you talking about? Who wants to speak to me? Who are you?" Coco asked, trying to place where she had seen this man before. Suddenly, an ice-cold chill ran down her spine.

It wasn't that she recognized *this* man, but more that she knew who he represented. He was from the dreaded Tonton Macoute, Haiti's notorious Secret Police. She turned to run and she wanted to scream.

A tremendous bolt of lightning exploded over the town, at that moment, the lights flickered, and went out. A moment later they flickered on and the door way was empty. Coco and the man were gone.

Jack was watching Coco when the lightning struck. He caught the frozen image of her struggling with two men, just as the lights went out. At first, he thought the booze was playing tricks on his mind, but when the lights came back on, Coco was, definitely, gone. "What the hell," he said, hurrying over to the door and out into the street, looking left and right for any sign of her.

At that moment, the sky opened and rain poured down in blinding sheets, soaking him to the skin. Jack saw movement and ran towards Bahamas Street, shielding his eyes. A shadow materialized out of the dark and tripped him. He fell, hitting his chin on the rough pavement, and rolled, just as a shoe came down hard on his shoulder. Jack grabbed the foot and twisted. A loud crack sounded, followed by a scream of pain. Jack rolled left, coming up fast with balled fists, and began to pummel the shadow. Jack had the man bent over in pain. He stepped back and kicked the man in the face. The man snapped back and fell to the ground. Before Jack could move, someone hit him with a tremendous blow to the side of his head and he went down, stunned.

"Shoot him. We must leave here, immediately," a voice called out.

Jack shook his head and forced himself to get up. He was on his knees when his head cleared. He was looking down the barrel of a pistol held by a man, silhouetted by the street light. The rain poured down on him. It was over, no more running.

"*Mon ami*, I am sorry," the shadow said, as he pulled the trigger.

Jack saw the muzzle flash and then there was darkness. He fell over on his side, unaware of his life's blood mixing with the storm gutter's runoff.

Chapter 5

A tall thin man stood, unseen, in the watery shadows, watching Jack's head snap to the side from the gunshot; watching him fall back into the gutter, flopping his arms over his head. He watched as the shooter and another man helped their injured comrade up and into the car and speed away. He could see Coco in the back seat, still struggling with her kidnappers. Lightning flashed overhead lighting up the street. Someone was running towards the wounded man, calling out something which was lost in the rumbling of thunder. Soon, two more men were running towards the downed figure.

"Jack! Jack! Talk to me.! Someone call 911, hurry, he's bleeding!" Lamont yelled.

"What happened to him?"

"I don't know. I saw him run up the street. Then, I heard a shot and saw a car disappear down Bahamas Street. Call the cops."

The thin man shivered from the cold rain, as he huddled back in the shadows. His heart was beating painfully in his chest. He placed a tiny nitro pill under his tongue. He was too late to warn Coco of the danger she was in. He had watched two men pulling her, while she was screaming and fighting, not three feet past where he hid. He could have reached out and touched them, as they ran by. He had the chance to help Coco, but he slinked back in fear instead, afraid of what these men were capable of doing.

Henrí Gastón was still terrified from the years he had spent in Fort Dimanche at the hands of the Tonton Macoute under François 'Papa Doc' Duvalier, the President-For-Life of Haiti. He wiped tears from his eyes at the memory of him and his wife escaping Haiti, along with Renee Duvalier and her baby daughter, Simone 'Coco' Duvalier, thirty years earlier when Jean-Claude 'Baby Doc' Duvalier assumed power after his father had died. Following his father's example, the first month of his reign as President-For-Life, Baby Doc had killed over two hundred senior military and police officers, along with dozens of diplomats and bureaucrats suspected of treason and plotting against the regime. Even close family and friends disappeared. In the process, he had killed his sister Renee's lover, a minor captain of the palace guard, and forced her and her bastard child to flee Haiti, penniless with only the clothes on their backs and a small pasteboard suitcase. Henrí Gaston's wife, Lucinda, had been Renee's nanny since childhood and was exiled along with Renee and Baby Coco. The real reason Henrí had been sent to prison was that he had been a butler and waiter in the household for years, but was found to be lazy and lacking in his zeal to serve Papa Doc and the Duvalier household. He was charged with treason. Upon the death of Papa Doc, as a show of mercy, Renee's brother, Jean-Claude, aka 'Baby Doc', released Henrí from prison to accompany the women into exile. The small group of exiles left Haiti on a forty-six-foot schooner, loaded with one-hundred and fifty other refugees from the Tonton Macoute's murderous rampage across the countryside, killing and murdering under the tyrannical approving eye of Baby Doc. Three days out of Port-O-Prince, a storm tore off the mainsail, snapped the mast, and drowned a hundred of the refugees. Coco's mother was one of the unlucky ones who drowned. Henrí, Lucinda, and Baby Coco, finally, made their way via the Bahamas, to the slums of Little Haiti north of Miami where Coco was raised in poverty.

The terror that he felt tonight, being so close to the Tonton Macoute thugs, was as frightening as his first night, when he was arrested and charged with treason and of having suspicious thoughts against the president. That night, Papa Doc's Bogeymen had castrated him with a machete and left him to bleed to death. He had almost died from blood loss and the infection that followed, but somehow, he lived, only to be tortured, periodically, at the hands of the Tonton Macoute. Before qualifying as a political refugee in the United States, he was required to have an extensive medical exam. The exam revealed an absence of both left and right thumbs, missing fingernails and toenails, an empty eye socket, his left eye missing, upper and lower teeth missing, deep cut and lash scars on his front and back torso, missing testicles, right knee shattered, the result of a gunshot, advanced malnutrition, and worms. Yes, he was very scared of the men he had come to Key West to warn Coco about, and he had failed. Now, she was their captive, and from what his sources in Haiti were saying, she was in mortal danger. The Bogeymen were on the move.

Chapter 6

Coco tried to free her her efforts and pulled her close, an evil grin on his face. She tried to pull her hand from the tight grip her captor had on her. The more she struggled, the tighter his grip became. The thug laughed at her resistance.

"Maybe, the Little One will let me have you, when he is finished with you. Would you like that, *Ma Cheri?* Would you like for André to show you his tricks?"

Without any warning, she gave a blinding head-butt to her tormentor that rocked him back against the SUV's door.

"You touch me and I'll kill you," Coco sneered, as she went for the man's eyes with her talon-like fingers extended. Her nails sunk into his fleshy cheeks and clawed downward, leaving a trail of deep trenches. As she sank her teeth into her target's ear, a blinding light exploded against the side of her head. She fell away from her opponent, shaking her head when a fist smashed her face, breaking her nose, several harsh blows to her ribs knocked the wind out of her and she rolled up into a ball, not able to catch her breath. Rough hands beat and smashed her face and head, while other hands tore at her clothes. Coco screamed in agony, her breasts were squeezed in an iron grip, twisting and pulling. It felt like they were being torn off. There was a moment of respite from the agony, as the man let go of her breasts, but just as suddenly, a mighty blow hit her straight on, smashing the right breast flat on her chest. Her mind went blank and she lost consciousness.

Marcel Duvalier stood over Coco's bruised and beaten body for several minutes, trying mightily to control his anger. What lay before him was not the beautiful woman in the photos he had ordered discreetly taken over a period of time. All his life, he had been compared to this woman and her beauty. Marcel was a very ugly and hate filled man. His head was too large for his thin body, and was accentuated by bright yellow nappy hair, pink tinged blue eyes, and an overly large mouth, with gaps between his front teeth. Marcel was an albino, not unusual to be sure, among the ten million Haitian blacks. The difference was that Marcel was a psychopath and sadist with assumed power from his family name.

Since Marcel's father, Baby Doc's, return to Haiti, after twenty-five years of self-imposed exile, his goal had been to overthrow the current government and reinstate the Duvalier reign of terror over the island. Marcel worshipped his father and worked tirelessly in helping his father regain the presidency. When his father asked him to organize the old Tonton Macoute Secret Police, he jumped at the chance. Quickly, he realized he had an affinity for inflicting torture and murder, and soon, had the old terrorist gang up and running, spreading blood and fear into the hearts and minds of the Haitian people. No one who opposed his father was safe. Whole families would disappear, fortunes and riches were confiscated and shared among Baby Doc's followers. Marcel was extremely successful in dispensing jungle-style justice as Director of Internal Security within his father's organization, a government within a government. He was likened to his grandfather, Papa Doc himself. He was, soon, known as Little Doc, and everyone feared him, including his own father.

Among the newly resurrected Tonton Macoute, Marcel was, more affectionately, known as the Vampire. Marcel had gathered many in the old organization, who had thrived under his grandfather's and father's regimes, and gave each authority over different regions of the country to rebuild their paramilitary organizations, get rid of the current local officials, collect protection monies, which he called taxes, and to terrorize the local populations. At the heart of the terror campaign was the use of Voodoo spiritual worship and the Haitian's fear of the dead. Fully eighty percent of Haitians call themselves Catholics, but practice Voodoo, and the Tonton Macoute—which translates to Bogeymen—use this practice in their terror campaigns.

As he nibbled on a torn and bleeding fingernail, Marcel looked down at his cousin's beaten and battered body. He felt an unfamiliar, momentary, feeling of concern for her, rather than the lifelong hatred he held for her because of her and her mother's beauty, and his self-loathing for his ugliness. He had never known love himself, his father shunned him and avoided almost all contact with him as he was growing up. He was an embarrassment to the Duvalier family and was known behind his back as *Le Blanc Creole*.

Now, here was real beauty, a beauty that he had marveled when he was growing up. The times that he visited his grandfather's palace as a child, he would go through family photo albums, stare at old photos of his Aunt Renee, and admire her beauty. It was rumored that when grandfather died, his own father, Baby Doc, killed Aunt Renee's lover and banished her and her newborn daughter from the island, because of the shame she had brought on the family for taking a mixed Haitian man, rather than a true blooded descendent of Africa. Marcel found himself aroused as he looked at his cousin's partially nude body. He had never seen her in the flesh, only in surveillance photos taken over the years that he would secretly compare to her mother's photos. Coco Duvalier was the exact image of her mother, Renee. Even battered and injured, she had a presence about her of beauty and elegance with an aura of sexuality that attracted men. Marcel brushed at a tear and he shook himself out of his memories. The tear was the result of a chronic eye infection, rather than one of feelings. Several opponents in the past had mistaken his tearing for weakness only to their eternal regret. With a final thought of, perhaps, having his way with her before she disappeared forever, he ran his hand over her swollen and bruised breasts. Once he had the information he needed from her, she would be more of a liability than an asset to him and his father. Better yet, maybe, he would keep her as a plaything, tucked away in one of his villas in the mountains.

Marcel pulled his thoughts to the present and stared at the idiot who had disobeyed his orders.

"Is this the way you follow orders, André? Is this what I said I wanted you to do? To beat her, and rape her?" Marcel said, walking around the table Coco was placed on.

"*Non*, Monsieur. She became like a wild woman and we were forced to subdue her," André answered. "Not to worry, Monsieur, she is still alive. A few broken bones perhaps, a scar or two…"

Marcel pulled his pistol as he approached André, and shot him in the forehead from only a few inches away. The force of the round pushed André's body across the basement room and against the wall. The smoke from the round lingered in wisps as the others in the room held their breath, waiting to see if Little Doc was going to shoot each of them.

"Get this *mérde* out of my sight," Marcel growled. "Charles, get the consulate doctor down here to care for Mademoiselle Duvalier. Philippe, come with me."

Chapter 7

Max Simms stuffed the last couple of inches of the jerked beef stick into his mouth and chewed. His Adam's apple and clip-on bowtie bounced rhythmically with each swallow. Bull Drummond absently watched the action thinking that the shirt collar was excessively tight to allow anything to pass down Max's skinny chicken neck. If anything, it would get lodged in his throat and he would be damned if he was going to give him more than a hard whack to the back to clear it. Mouth to mouth just wasn't going to happen. He watched as Max ran a boney finger around his collar, crisis averted.

"Bull, I can't put it together. Who would want to kidnap Coco, except maybe some deranged rapist? And right from under our noses! I'm telling you it don't make sense."

"Nah, it wasn't any rapist. My money is on some boyfriend issues from the past…"

"Bullshit, the only boyfriend she's had since I've known her is Major Price, and, as far as I know, they're all lovey-dovey, thinking of tying the knot. Besides, he wouldn't shoot Marsh in the process. Nah, we're talking sex deviate here."

Both men winced at the sudden flash of lightning across the hospital room's window, followed by a loud clap of thunder that shook the windowpane. It was after six in the morning, Hurricane Misty had stalled over the Keys. It was predicted to sit and spin for the next twelve to twenty-four hours. Bull cracked his knuckles, as he ran through a mental checklist of things that he did to prepare the *Island Queen* for the storm, seeing if he had overlooked anything. The *Queen* was a sixty-four-foot salvage boat that he captained for Jack. He loved it better than any woman he had ever met. He was comforted knowing that she was safely tied off to a buoy in the Key West channel, with a storm anchor out and her decks secured. After twenty-six years in the blue water Navy, he knew how to set a storm anchor, by God, and the *Queen* wasn't going anywhere, unless he was at the helm. He cracked his knuckles again. His sea green eyes squinted from years of watching the horizon for trouble.

"Maybe, there's more to this than we think, Max. There are some strange people down here. Remember the bodies they found a few months ago, shoved down that septic tank over on Shark Key? The place belonged to a rich guy up in Miami. Come to find out, he's a weekend predator. Snuffed kids for the hell of it. Grabbed 'em off the streets and *poof,* gone. No sex, no nothing, just strangled 'em."

"Jeez, Bull, don't talk about that kind of stuff. Gives me the squirts, just thinking about somebody grabbing me by the neck," Max said, as he massaged his throat. "I drove a cab in

Manhattan for thirty-five years and my biggest fear was some punk reaching around and cutting me from ear to ear for a few dollars."

"Is that why you wear those heavy-duty starched shirts and the phony bowtie, to protect your neck?"

"Bull, you being Navy and all probably don't understand this, but when you work with the public, you have to look sharp. Me, I'm a public servant-like person, so, I should look extra nice. There ain't nothing better looking than a clean white short-sleeved shirt, bowtie, pressed trousers and black wingtips. The passengers like their drivers to look neat. Makes 'em feel safe, and they tip better."

"A real Madison Avenue approach to driving a fucking hack, huh?"

"Hey, fuck you! I got cabbie of the year once. Bloomberg, himself, gave it to me, plus tickets to the fights at the Garden for a year…"

"Shut up! Whoever it is talking, just shut up. My head is killing me," Jack croaked, loudly.

"Jackie, you're alive! Thank God! We've been worried sick about you," Max said, grabbing Marsh's hand. "You okay? Want some water? Gotta take a leak, a couple of mints?"

"Max, take it easy, let him come around, give him some breathing room for Christ's sake."

Jack licked his lips, "Water."

Bull placed the straw in Jack's mouth and held it, as he took small amounts.

"Am I alive?"

"Nah, we're the last two virgins. You already polished off the first seventy," Max laughed. "The bad news is that Bull's number seventy-one. The good news, I'm last, and I'm no flip-flopper, so you're getting off easy."

"Somebody shoot me, put me out of my misery, save me from these two clowns," Jack whispered. "My head feels like a wrecking ball hit it. What's with the swami wrap?" Jack asked, running his hands, carefully, over his head.

"The mutt that shot you wasn't such a good shot. He probably jerked the trigger instead of squeezing, and it threw him off a couple of inches."

"So, if this guy was such a bad shot, why do I feel like Iron Mike just nailed me?"

"The bullet dug a trench down the side of your head, Jackie. Lots of blood, stitches, ergo the swami wrap. You have a mild concussion, too, that the doc is monitoring, but you should be up and out of here in a couple of days."

"Ergo! Ergo! Max, you've been working the TIMES crossword puzzle, while I'm lying here dying," Jack croaked, loudly. "Meanwhile, where the hell is Coco? Is she alive? Do we know who snatched her…?"

"Jeez, Jackie, take it easy. You're going to get a blood clot or something. Look at your face, its turning blue. Relax and let Bull update you, okay? Sheesh, a guy tries to improve himself and look what he gets?"

Jack flopped back down on his pillow, breathing deep, forcing himself to relax. Max was right. Getting all upset is not what was needed now. He needed to be calm, be prepared for any bad news Bull was going to share with him. If Coco was dead or hurt bad, he'd make it up to her, somehow. This was entirely his fault.

"Bull, give it to me straight up, don't hold back. I can handle it. Mano-a-mano-like, old buddy. How bad was it? Did they make her suffer?"

Bull looked down, shuffling his feet, "Jack, I'll be honest," he paused, "…we don't know shit."

"*What!* What do you mean you don't know shit? Is she alive, dead, what?'

"I'm telling you, we don't know anything, other than someone shot you, jumped in a car with Coco and took off. We don't have any leads, any suspects, any motive, nada. We're just damn glad you didn't get yourself killed," Bull said.

"What about the cops? Are they working on it?"

"Nope, Sheriff Taylor says until Coco's been missing twenty-four hours, he can't do anything. We will have to go in and file a missing person's complaint..."

"What about this?" Jack pointed to his head, "Doesn't this carry any weight? I was two inches away from being meat."

"Taylor and a couple of deputies looked up and down the street for a shell casing, or anything else that might help, but didn't spend more than ten minutes on the scene," Bull said.

"Jackie, the man doesn't like you. I heard him say to one of the deputies that it was too bad the shooter didn't finish the job, now the ball was back in his court. Can you believe that, coming from an elected official? The man should be impeached or something..."

"I wouldn't expect less from Taylor. I know he and his deputies are on the take from every bar and shop owner, up and down Duval, except for me. Hell, even the working girls kick back to him. The man is a crook, and he has it in for me because I won't play his game. That's why he's not wasting anytime or manpower on Coco."

The three men sat in silence as the storm raged outside. The only facts they had to go on were that two men had kidnapped Coco from the Sand Bar, Jack saw them and gave chase, being shot in the process. At least four men had been involved. Jack broke or sprained one's ankle, one shot Jack, another called from the car, and, probably, a fourth drove the car. The big unknown was who were they? Why did they take a chance like that and snatch Coco in plain sight of the bar patrons?

"Hear me out on this," Jack said, breaking the silence. "These aren't local mutts. No one down here would ever try that with someone like Coco. She's too well-known, and besides, she doesn't have any enemies in town that I know of. These bums had to be from the mainland. They were all black men, maybe Bahamian, or more likely Haitian. The one that shot me apologized in French before pulling the trigger..."

"That cuts it down to about half the Caribbean population, Jack. I like where you're going with this, though, but what was their motive? Coco is a one-of-a-kind beauty, for sure, but Miami is filled with beauties. There has to be a reason that they snatched *her*," Bull offered.

"Once a month Coco takes off Saturday afternoon, catches the Greyhound to Miami, and then returns Sunday night," Jack said. "She never offers up any details or what the purpose of her trips is. I never asked, just figuring she needed a few hours away from the Sand Bar's craziness. This has to be tied to something she does in Miami."

"Hey, a few months back, I gave her a lift in my cab. She didn't get away until late and missed the bus, so, I figured I could shoot her a low fare to cover gas and still make a few bucks on the trip. I took her up to some dump in Little Haiti, north of Miami, and dropped her off," Max said. "You ever been there? The neighborhood was like being in Port-au-Prince, signs and everything's in that Frenchie-Creole lingo, fruit carts, street venders, people walking around with shit stacked on their heads, motor scooters with five people on 'em, just like you see on the Natural Geographic Channel. The only thing missing was dirt streets, but there were plenty of potholes, deep enough to swallow a family riding one of them rice burners. Yeah, and Voodoo stuff all over the place. I was sitting at a red light and this guy was trying to sell me a cigarette out of a pack. I told him to scram, he blew some kind of red powdery crap at me, and shook a fucking chicken foot at me, screaming something. I hunched down, hit the gas, and got the hell out of there. I had migraines, for a few days after that…"

"Are you through with the travelogue?" Jack asked. "If so, can we get along with the business of finding Coco?"

"That's what I'm saying, Jackie. I remember how to get to that place. We can start there. Bull and me will run up there and ask whoever answers the door if they know anything about Coco's whereabouts. If they play dumb, we smack 'em around a little bit. What ya say?"

"I like the part about asking, but the smacking around might be a little much…at least, until we know what we're up against. If this is the place where you dropped Coco off, we shouldn't anticipate any trouble," Jack said, thinking through Max's idea. It wasn't much of a plan, but sometimes that is the best kind. He remembered reading about General Patton's theory that "A poor plan executed boldly was better than a superior plan timidly implemented." Then again, his Marine training taught him to *improvise, adapt, and overcome,* and if that failed, run like hell.

"Before we talk about running up to Miami, let's make sure that Coco's not being held around town here," Jack said. "Max, run over to Coco's apartment and see what you can find out. Ask her neighbors if they have seen her. Talk to the manager about any strangers asking about her. The key to her apartment is in the cash register behind the bar. Ask Lamont to pass it over to you."

"You want me to toss the place, see what I can find?" Max asked.

"Max, just go in, see if she is there, feel the stove, dishes, look to see if her bed has been slept in, check the shower, washcloths, and bath towels to see if they are wet, smell for fresh scents of her. That kind of stuff, but don't tear the place up, ya knucklehead."

"Bull, see the grief I take from this guy? Treats me like a shmuck. Ask him who saved his ass against that fucking Russian mafia guy, or the broad that was after him with the ice pick? Who taught him three-card monty...?"

"Max, snap out of it," Jack said. "My head can't take much more of that whiney voice. Bull, why don't you ride over with him? Keep him out of trouble, then come back here and pick me up."

"You can't leave, Jack. What about the concussion? You're in no shape to be up and around, much less if we get into a rumble," Bull said.

"I'll talk to the doctor. If he thinks it's too risky, I'll stay behind. Believe me, I don't want to be walking around with my head pounding like this either. Let's see what he says and then we'll decide what to do, OK?"

Chapter 8

Marcel Duvalier's face was contorted in rage when he slammed down the telephone in the Council General's office. It was after 9:00 a.m., and he stood across the desk from his political ally and friend, Ambrose Sachál, Haiti's Consulate General in Miami. The two men had become close, over time, as they both discovered their mutual enjoyment of brutality and battery to young girls, and occasionally boys. Although Ambrose was an employee of the current Haitian government and President, his loyalties lay with the Duvalier family and their effort to regain control of the country. There was a growing conspiracy within the senior ranks of the Haitian government to overthrow the U.S. lackey, Martin Robespierre, from the Presidency and reinstate Jean-Claude 'Baby Doc' Duvalier as President-For-Life. It would be like the old days when loyalists became rich and powerful, especially with the billions of dollars in aid pouring in after the earthquakes and storms of recent years. "Drink this, Marcel, you must calm yourself. Whatever it was your father said to you is not worth you having a stroke over. Please, sit down and drink this water," Ambrose fawned.

"That idiot wants me to send the girl to him. He is worried that I will get carried away and kill her before we find out where the information is. This is the end, Ambrose. He as much said that I was to back away from any further involvement with the search for grandmamma's hidden accounts. I swear someday, I will kill him," Marcel stammered. "I hate him, I tell you, I despise the fat pig."

"Easy, friend," Ambrose cautioned, moving his fingers to his lips. "Your father has a long reach. Even here, he has his eyes and ears. Do not say foolish things that can be used by the Tonton.

"The Tonton are loyal to me, Ambrose, no one else. They would never turn against me," Marcel said.

"Ambrose, make the necessary arrangements for our guest to fly to Port-au-Prince on the Consulate's plane. She may not be in any shape to fly commercial. Notify His Excellency that I will comply with his wishes. I may fly along with her. It depends on what I learn from her in the next few hours."

"Of course, Marcel. As you wish."

Marcel knocked softly on the door, then entered, without waiting for an answer. The basement room was small, with a bed in the corner, two chairs, and a table with a lamp on it.

Consulate personnel used the room to rest when working security shifts. Coco was moved to the room last night when the doctor arrived to tend her injuries. This morning she was seated at the table with her head resting on her arms, dozing in and out from the pain pills the doctor had given her. Not fully awake, but in pain.

Coco gasped loudly. Her hand flew to her mouth in surprise as Marcel entered and hurried toward her. She stood and backed tight against the wall ready to fend off any more beatings.

"Sit, please sit. I am here to talk with you. I mean you no harm," Marcel coaxed.

"Who are you? Or better yet, what are you?" she asked, as she recoiled from his touch. Coco had seen an occasional albino around Little Haiti, but they were shunned out of fear of their mystical powers they were believed to possess. Growing up, her aunt often told stories of Voodoo spiritual leaders in Haiti who were albino, dwarfs, or deformed in some manner by the spirit gods and cast soul-stealing spells on those not watching for devils. And this creep fit the description.

Marcel threw his head back and laughed an insane cackle "Oh, that is good, Dear Cousin. What am I? Yes, that is the question. Perhaps, you and I can solve the mystery of the Duvalier's curse on its sons and daughters."

"What are you talking about? You are crazy, aren't you? Why did you kidnap me? What do you want from me?" Coco kept her eyes and face averted from Marcel's gaze. *'Never look a Voodoo Priest directly in the eye,'* her aunt had cautioned.

"Coco, please, relax. I am not going to cast a spell on you. We only have a little time before you leave, so, we must not waste time on childish tales," Marcel said, sitting down at the table. He sighed, "Where to begin? It's true, I am your cousin. Your mother, Renee is my father's sister. I was born after your mother and you left Haiti, but I have seen her pictures often over the years. I have always thought she was the most beautiful woman I had ever seen. That is until I saw pictures of you…"

"Pictures of me? How did you see pictures of me? I was a baby when we left Haiti. I have lived in Miami all my life." Coco sat down across from Marcel, but kept her eyes averted.

"My father is insane. When he assumed the presidency after our grandfather died, he went on a killing spree, wiping out whole families of friends and relatives, taking their property and wealth. He had your father killed, only because he had a trace of white French blood in his veins, and my father couldn't accept that in his lust for African purity among the Haitian people. He banished your mother from the homeland because of you being the unborn child of tainted blood." Marcel licked his lips unconsciously, deep in thought.

"It has always been rumored that my father was secretly in love with your mother, his sister, and the real reason he killed your father and banished your mother was because he knew he could never have her." Marcel had a lopsided wicked grin. "Or, perhaps, my father did have his way with your mother, and we are brother and sister." Marcel threw his head back in an obnoxious braying laugh. "Think of that, my pretty, you and I out of the same poisoned womb, sired by a goat."

"You're crazy. My mother drowned at sea when we were making the crossing. My aunt and uncle raised me here in Miami and they never mentioned any of this to me," Coco said, in disbelief.

"Believe me, my dear Cousin, everything I am telling you is true. Ah, but it gets better, Ma Chere. It seems our dearest grandmamma was also an unscrupulous bit of work. Behind her sweet smile, she was undermining her own husband. Stealing the old man's fortune as fast as he was stealing it from the national treasury. The old bitch cleaned him out. Our beloved grandfather, Papa Doc Duvalier, went to his grave with nothing in all those offshore accounts but air. It was believed that grandmamma had billions in hidden accounts around the Caribbean and South America when she died…and no one knows where any of it is hidden."

Coco was enraptured with these tales of her mother and father and the family she never knew in Haiti. Her aunt and uncle were the only family she had ever known. She knew little of them, other than from the occasional story auntie would tell about her mother. Now, here was this strangely deformed albino talking about a grandmother stealing billions of dollars from her powerful husband, an uncle who secretly loved her mother, and this newfound cousin confiding in her about all these dysfunctional people.

"What do you want from me?" Coco asked. "Why are you telling me all this?"

"First of all, I want you to call me Marcel. Whether you like it or not, we are blood relatives. My sins are visible for all to see. I am cursed with a hideous body that scares the most hardened among us. I have a raging devil inside of me that will not be denied. My father's sins are an insatiable lust for money and power. He hides them behind a mask of joviality and false care. Our grandfather was insane and evil itself, killing thousands just for the thrill of it. Some of the old Tonton still whisper about bonfires in the mountains where victims were slaughtered and eaten as Voodoo Priestesses chanted ancient rituals, and young virgins were sacrificed to the old gods of Africa." Marcel paused, wiping the white, bubbly spittle from the corners of his mouth.

"I don't want to hear anymore of all this insane talk. I am not part of that life. I have my own life and am very happy. So, if you will just give me a ride from wherever it is I am to a real doctor, I will get out of your life. You can carry on with all the palace intrigue," Coco said, as she gazed around the room, still not convinced that she was completely safe from the human frog who claimed to be her cousin.

"Oh, no, my dear Cousin. You and I still have much to discuss. It seems that grandmamma may have given your mother information about where she hid the old man's money. Your mother and grandmamma were said to be very close. When my father killed your father, the old bitch reportedly disowned her son and swore that she would do everything possible to destroy him. Wonder of wonders, shortly after this declaration, poor grandmamma up and died, while sitting in her garden, a trickle of blood running down her chin, but from no apparent cause. Many whispered that she had been killed by a spell cast by a very powerful witch doctor in the mountains, but who knows? These silly rumors of witch doctors and spirits and spells are all the workings of superstitious minds."

"You are scaring me, Marcel. I want to leave. If our grandmamma gave my mother information about the whereabouts of grandfather's money, then it went to her watery grave with her. I have always been told that we arrived with nothing but the clothes on our backs. In my case, nappies on my bottom. We had nothing when we arrived."

"See? That's where this story breaks down. We know from eyewitness accounts that the night your mother left, she had a small suitcase and a bundle with her. It was determined that the bundle was you, but the suitcase is an unknown. The other known is that your mother's nanny and her husband were commanded to leave with your mother and you. In a moment of paranoia, my father sent the two people along with her, thinking that he could turn the old couple against her, if it were ever necessary."

"I think your father is a very evil person and I really don't want anything to do with him …or his son. So, if you don't mind, I'll be leaving now," Coco said, as she stood and walked toward the door.

Marcel was enraged at this disrespect. No one ever talked to him that way, and never just walked away! He grabbed a chair and swung with all his might, hitting Coco squarely in the back. She flew forward and collapsed, gagging for breath. Marcel knelt down on her neck and bounced.

"Don't ever talk to me that way again, you bitch. I give the orders. I decide who comes and goes, and I decide if you live or die. Do you understand me?" He bounced harder causing her head to slam into the floor, "Do you understand? Answer me!"

"Yes…yes, I understand. Please, stop."

Marcel stood and kicked her hard in the ribcage. Coco rolled up into a ball of searing pain.

"Now, listen to me. We are taking a trip to your uncle's hovel in Little Haiti and you are going to show me all your mother's possessions, anything that your aunt or you kept over the years. You will show me everything, or you will die. I would enjoy cutting your stomach, letting you bleed to death, but I need you for now. Now, get off the floor, we have things to do."

Chapter 9

Breakfast smells mixing with the normal antiseptic hospital smells made Jack's mouth water...a sure sign that he was going to be okay. After a few quick splashes of water in all the strategic places, and a shave, he was feeling human again. The huge bandage wrap around his head was still awkward, but the throb from the wound underneath was almost unnoticeable, unless he lowered or moved it too quickly. Same with his vision. If he didn't move too quickly, everything was where it was supposed to be. But, if he moved too fast, two and three of everything would dance across his line of sight, then, slowly, refocus. He recalled having the same crazy dizzy sensation as a kid the time he and a friend chugged down a quart of Mogen David grape wine on a dare.

"How many fingers am I holding up, Mr. Marsh?" Dr. Laura Summers asked.

"Seven."

"I'm serious, how many?"

"Three."

"That's better. Not correct, but closer," she said, scribbling something on Jack's chart.

"I think we can release you, but, only if you take it easy. No exercising, manual labor, alcohol intake, and easy on the heavy foods for a few days," she ticked off, as she thumped Jack's knees for a reaction, and then listened to his breathing.

As the doctor had her head down listening intently to his heart, Jack caught a glimpse of cleavage through the lab coat and blouse. An immediate flash of cognizance from his upper brain to his lower brain told him that a female of the species was close by. Both brains snapped to attention, alert for opportunity. He knew at that point that he was going to be all right. No problemo.

"Doc, give it to me straight. Will I recover and be a normal functioning member of society?" Jack asked, with a straight face. "Or, should I start getting my affairs in order?"

"Don't be a smart ass, Mr. Marsh. I have read your medical history and according to our records, this is your third concussion, in as many years. Not to mention the broken bones, a couple of gunshot wounds, and both major and minor cuts to the torso and limbs," she said. "You're a regular curiosity among our junior staff, but, I know you for what you are. I know all the local stories about Jack Marsh, the town's macho man, always poking his nose where it doesn't belong...and coming away with it broken, more often than not. Among the normal residents, you're seen as just one more of life's losers, who rolls into town, makes a few bucks, then disappears overnight to parts unknown. But, down on Duval Street, you're the hero of the moment, the macho de jure, loved and looked up to by all the other losers."

"That's me. Jack, the giant slayer. Like they say though, life's a bitch and she'll take you to the wall if you let her. I've been to the wall a couple of times and I didn't like it. If you're ever down on Duval, stop by. I'll buy you a drink and tell you stories about the *losers,* as you call them. I think you'll come away with a different point of view," Jack said. "It's been a long night, and it's shaping up to be an even longer day. With your permission, I would like to be released and make way for some other patient who needs this space. I know the routine and promise to take it as easy as I can."

"Whatever. Just be careful, Mr. Marsh. I don't want to see you back in here for a while. Try and stay out of trouble. Next time duck…or run."

"I'm an Olympic style sprinter when it comes to my safety, Doc. Don't worry, I won't be back.

Max answered his cell phone on the first ring,

"Island Taxi, at your service."

"Max, it's me, Jack. They cut me loose a few minutes ago. Where are you guys?"

"I'll be at your location in less than five minutes. Can you be outside at the curb or do you want me to come in?"

"I'll be outside. How did it go at Coco's apartment?"

"The place was trashed, Jackie, even the toilet paper was unrolled. You wouldn't believe the way they tore everything up. The good news is that we caught an old geezer hiding in one of the closets, so scared he peed himself. Says he's Coco's uncle. Says he saw the whole thing last night. Says he knows who snatched her. Bull believes him, but not me, though. These island people will lie about anything. When I was driving a hack in the city, they would even lie to me about where they wanted to go. That happened, I would just pull over to the curb and tell 'em to scram…"

"Ok, Ok, I get the picture. I'll be down front waiting," Jack said, shaking his head as he hung up. *"Too much fucking information, Max,"* he mumbled, sticking his wallet in his pocket, counting the bills first out of habit.

The floor nurse insisted that Jack ride out in a wheelchair, more to cover the hospital from a liability suit than concern for the patient.

Doctor Summers called out as he was being wheeled by the nurses' station,

"Mr. Marsh, I might take you up on your offer of free drinks," she said, with a hint of a smile.

"Mi casa, su casa. Just give me a head's up so I can hide the cheap stuff before you get there," Jack said, with a grin and a wink that shot a sliver of pain to his eyelid, making it flutter rapidly, several times. *"So much for the macho image,"* he muttered.

"Pardon, Sir?" the nurse said.

"Nothing. Let's roll."

Chapter 10

Max pulled his taxi out of the rain under the hospital's portico just as Jack was being wheeled out the double doors. Quickly, he set the emergency brake and ran around to open the sliding side door to help Jack climb aboard.

"Watch your step, Jackie," Max cautioned, as he balanced Jack unsteadily. "Honest to God, Jack. This is not a good idea for you to be out of the hospital. What happens if something goes crazy in your head and you croak, or something worse, while you're in my cab? They'll yank my permit for sure this time. Then what am I going to do? This is the only thing I'm trained for..."

"Shut up and let's get out of here. I'll be fine. Besides, I know how much you have stashed away, you old miser. You could buy and sell each one of us several times over," Jack said.

Max turned to the nurse.

"Here, sugar, buy yourself something pretty," he said, handing her a folded five-dollar bill.

"What's this for?" the nurse asked, looking at the money.

"A tip, doll. Little something for yourself. You know, for rolling the boss out."

"*Are you serious*? Shove this where the sun don't shine, you ignoramus," she said, and threw the bill in his face, turned, and stomped off.

"What!" Max exclaimed, confused by what had just happened. "Jeez, fucking women in the work force. Whatcha gonna do?" Max bent and retrieved the bill from the wet pavement and wiped it on his trouser leg, still baffled by someone not accepting a tip for services rendered.

Without a word, Jack settled into the center bench seat and turned to see Bull and the guy claiming to be Coco's uncle. Both men nodded greetings but, otherwise, remained silent.

"I hear that you are Coco's uncle. Is that correct?" Jack asked.

Before answering, the man looked over to Bull Drummond for approval to speak. Bull nodded his head,

"Go ahead. Just remember what I told you. If you're lying, I'll cut your gizzard out, old man."

"I have no reason to lie. I have told you the truth. I am who I say I am, and my niece is in serious trouble. I think I am already too late to save her," the old man sighed. "Mr. Marsh, you don't know me, but I know all about you, and how you helped my Coco over the past few years. Surely, God pointed her to you that night. You will never know the existence we suffered, until you came into our lives…"

"Hold on, you need to explain that. What do you mean by *our* lives?"

"The job, the steady income, the future. You got her off the street, and gave her respectability, and I thank you every

51

day of my life for that. At that time, my poor wife was diagnosed with cancer, I couldn't find work, and Coco was prostituting herself out to the scum of Miami each night, bringing in as much as she could for her auntie's treatments, but, it was never enough. At least, we knew we could be sure of a steady income, once you hired her to work in your establishment."

Jack was struck with this man's sincerity, also embarrassed for the good things being attributed to him, things he had no knowledge of.

Jack reached across the back of the seat with his hand out, "I'm Jack Marsh, Sir, and you are?"

"I am Henrí Gastón, of Little Haiti in North Miami. Before that, my home was Port-au-Prince," he said, shaking his mangled hand in Jack's.

Jack felt the deformity and looked down, "I'm sorry, I didn't notice. Would you prefer shaking with your other hand?"

Henrí laughed and held up his other hand, "Which would *you* prefer, Monsieur?"

Max drove slowly down Roosevelt, keeping an eye on the flooded street, and the other eye on crazy tourists on rented motorbikes. It was not even 8 a.m. yet, and these crazy nuts were out in the middle of a hurricane, playing dodge ball on wheels. The city's drain system couldn't keep up with the deluge and the streets were running one to two feet over the curbs. Max took it slow through the heavy downpour, as he avoided palm fronds, debris, and trash floating in the streets.

"So, Coco's real name is Simone, and her grandfather was Papa Doc Duvalier, President of Haiti. Her uncle, Baby Doc Duvalier killed her father and banished her mother from Haiti, because of her indiscretion with a mixed blood palace guard. And, on top of all that, her cousin, Marcel 'Little Doc' Duvalier, current head of the murderous Tonton Macoute Secret Police, has kidnapped Coco…I mean Simone, because he believes she knows where her grandmother hid her grandfather's stolen millions…"

"Billions, Monsieur, not millions," Henrí said, from the back seat.

"OK, billions then," Jack said, continuing the summary of what the old man had told them. "And, Coco never knew anything about the rumor of her grandmother passing the location of the money to her daughter before she was forced to leave Haiti. Is this correct? Do I have it all together?"

"Yes, Mr. Marsh. I would say that you have the gist of the story."

"Mr. Gastón, I hate to be a doubter, but that's, probably, the most preposterous story I have ever heard. Because Coco's last name is Duvalier doesn't mean she is, or ever was, heir apparent to anything. I think we have to dig deeper for something more plausible," Jack said, doubting the man's story and not really sure where this man fit in Coco's disappearance.

"Monsieur, you must believe me. It is all true, and if we don't do something quickly, I am afraid Simone will disappear. My guess is that if she is not already dead, then she soon will be. The Vampire is not known for his patience; the man is completely mad."

"Jack, we don't have any other leads. I say we go to work on what Henrí is saying. If it leads to something at all, it would be better than just sitting here waiting for her to turn up," Bull said.

"Monsieur Marsh, I have an idea that might free Simone. It will be very dangerous, and it will most assuredly bring the enemy to us. It could even cost us our lives, if we hesitate. We will need to be bold and courageous. Once we take the first step, we must be prepared to fight.

"Damn it, Gastón, quit with the scare tactics and spit it out," Jack said, frustrated with all the warnings of why it might be too dangerous to save Coco. "What's your plan?"

"Simple, *mon ami*. We call Marcél."

Jack and Bull exchanged glances, "And?"

"And, we tell him we will trade the hidden account information for the safe return of Simone," he said, simply.

"Are you saying that the story about the grandmother stealing her husband's money is real...and, that she gave the location to her daughter?" Jack said, excitedly. "Billions in stolen money, missing for almost forty years, and you know where it is?"

The cab came to a sliding stop, as Max pulled to the curb and swung around staring at Gastón.

"Yes, it is true, and yes, I know where the information is. But, it is not true that I know where the accounts are. I only know where the numbers are."

"You mean you've been sitting on this information for all these years and you never tried to find out where the money was?" Jack exclaimed. "Coco was raised in poverty, even worked as a prostitute to survive, when she could have had access to all that wealth. Why, Henrí, why didn't you find it?"

"Monsieur Marsh, you have no idea what it is like to be tortured, or the fear of knowing if you said the wrong thing, your family would disappear. Living in Miami is no different from living in Haiti. The Tonton are everywhere. There is no safety anywhere for any of us. They know who I am, where I live. They decide who makes a living and who does not, or who lives and who dies. Look at me, Monsieur, look at my hands, look at my eye, my teeth…my dead wife. Yes, I am afraid, Monsieur. The only way I was allowed to make a living was selling newspapers on the corner, or cigarettes to motorists. Even then, I had to pay them every week for the privilege of working and living. Don't condemn me for being weak. I hate them with a passion and would kill them with my bare hands…if I had hands."

"I'm sorry, Henrí," Jack said, feeling ashamed for being so quick to chastise the man for the way Coco had been raised. "Henrí, don't you think they will hunt you down and kill you for trying to bargain with them? They might return Coco to us, but you and she will never be safe again."

"Yes, this is true. I do not care for my own safety. I am old and have a bad heart. It is Coco that I care about. I must save her from those people. I promised my wife I would never let anything happen to her. We must hurry, Mr. Marsh, time is running out."

"Do you have the account information on you, or is it written down somewhere? We need that in our hands before we call anyone. That would be a sure way to get ourselves killed…going to a meet-up and not have our end of the swap."

"The information is in a very special place that I believe is safe, even from the Tonton thugs."

"Then let's go get it. Rather than call this Marcel character, we'll go see him."

Chapter 11

Max's pink taxi stuck out like a zit on a homecoming queen, as he threaded his way through the clog of mini cars, mini trucks, mini motor scooters, and the odd big luxury car. Throngs of people filled the sidewalks, storefront shops, and alleys, spilling over into the streets of Little Haiti. Bicycles loaded with goods and carts piled high with tropical fruits and vegetables added to the slow-moving flow as hawkers yelled out in English, French, and Creole. The people were poor. Their faces had the looks of fear and anticipation, as they flitted through the crowds. Nothing ever good happened to these people and they were always on the alert for trouble or danger. Out of all the towns in the Caribbean, there are none as rundown as Little Haiti in North Miami, except perhaps Port-au-Prince itself.

"These are my people, Jack. There is probably less than ten dollars among that crowd standing by that fruit stand…including the vender," Henrí said. "See the two men with the sunglasses, knit hats, and open shirts? Those are two of Marcel's Tonton tax collectors. If they think you have a dollar, or even loose change, they will tax you right then. If you refuse, they beat you, and take it anyway."

"Where's the Miami PD? Don't they patrol this area?"

Henrí laughed. "The police never come in here, even the fire fighters don't come in. If a house or shop catches fire, it's up to the people to put it out. If people get hurt or die, nobody outside cares. Babies are born here and old people die here. The only thing that keeps us alive is our faith in Bondyè, our Voodoo god, and his Loa spirit helpers. We have learned to trust no one for help, Jack. All these folks risked their lives to get away from the curse of Haiti, only to find themselves no better off than when they left."

"Curse? What are you talking about, what curse?" Max was holding his throat protectively, as he asked.

"Yes, Haiti's cursed. So many people have been killed or left to die that the whole country is nothing but a graveyard. They say that you can pick a spot and dig and you are going to run into somebody's bones. It's been that way for hundreds of years," Henrí said, studying the reactions he saw on his audience's faces. "Going back to the slaves' rebellion against their French masters, Haiti's been cursed. The story is that the leaders of the revolution made a pact with the devil for freedom from the cruel French. They sold the people's souls for all time, in return for freedom. Since then, the devil has sent plagues, storms, earthquakes, evil spirits, and death to the Haitian people. Even the dead are not left alone."

"That's all superstitious Voodoo crap. I'm not buying it," Max said, turning his attention back to the crowds of people.

"Mr. Simms, look around you. What do you see, what do you smell?" Henrí said. "I will tell you, my friend, it's fear you see and smell. Superstition you say? Maybe so, but how else can you explain their meager lives, if not for evil spirits? Now pull over and let me out."

"Hold on! Where do you think you're going?" Bull asked, as he put up a restraining hand.

"I am going to cut through that shop there, and take a peek at my house from the back, to make sure we are not walking into a trap. You stay in the car, until I signal you to come. Max, you stay with the car…"

"Uh-uh, I'm not staying here alone. I'm going with you guys," Max said, over his shoulder.

"If you leave your car alone, Max, there will be nothing left of it when we get back. Roll up the windows and lock the doors. I will send someone to watch over you and to chase away the thieves."

"Yeah, but, what about my person? What if they break in and try some of that Voodoo stuff on me? Maybe try and turn me into one of them zombie things you see on TV."

"Max, I wouldn't worry, if I was you. I think they only go after intelligent life forms. You should be okay," Jack said, smiling.

"Screw you guys. Sure, make fun, but, if I'm gone when you come back, it's your fault," Max said, as he swiveled his head around looking for trouble.

Henrí disappeared into the bodega's interior shadows as Jack and Bull checked their pistols, just in case there was trouble. The *snick* of a round being shuttled into a chamber gave Jack comfort.

"Let's hope things go smooth in there. Max, you stay put. If you hear any shooting, start this puppy up and be ready to haul ass out of here," Jack said.

"What if there's shooting and you guys don't come back? Am I supposed to just sit here and wait for those tom tom people to show up?"

"Don't worry, we'll be back…and you better be sitting here waiting. You're our ride out of here, Max. Don't let us down."

"Jackie, I ain't never left nobody hanging. Ask Lucky Giancano if I ever left him. Ask him who the best wheelman is who ever drove for him. Ask around the old neighborhood, they'll tell ya.

"You drove for Lucky Giancano?" Bull asked, impressed.

"Well…not directly. Actually, it was his cousin, but it was just as dangerous, believe me. One wrong move and they would have whacked me."

Ten minutes crawled by. Jack was getting concerned. Henrí should have been back by now, if he was just taking a quick peek.

"You two sit tight. I'll take a quick look-see," Jack said, and slid out the taxi's side door.

The small shop was dim inside. The only light came leaking in from the street. The small place was filled with cloth bags of rice, half barrels of beans, and shriveled vegetables of every description. Canned goods with strange names filled shelves. Housewares hung from the ceiling in clumps next to flypaper strips black with their catch which moved with a life of their own. Jack spotted a rack of colorful Rasta knit hats, grabbed one off its hook, and pulled it down over his swath of head bandages. A quick look in a cloudy hand mirror hanging next to the hats made him smile.

"That's ten dollars," an old shriveled crone said, hidden in a cloudbank of stinky cigar smoke.

Jack stepped over to the counter, which was nothing more than two boards laid across sawhorses. "Where did Mr. Gastón go? I am his friend. I think he may need my help."

"Bocor Gastón don't need your help. He have strong Ogua spirits with him," the woman said, as she puffed on some home-wrapped cigar.

Jack was getting dizzy from the heavy smell of smoke mixed with strange seasonings and odors he couldn't identify. His eye came to rest on a crucifix with a black Christ hanging upside down. Jars and canisters on crowded shelves filled the back wall of the room. Flickering light from votive candles made the old woman's wrinkled black face appear to be in constant motion. Jack saw movement in the shadows at the other end of the counter and leaned in closer. A large black dog was staring back at Jack, its hackles bristling, eyes like white-hot orbs. The dog's body appeared to be gyrating slowly, undulating from one shape to another.

Jack shook his head to clear it, "What the fuck!" Jack stepped back from the counter. "Call off your dog before he decides to lunge," Jack slurred.

The old woman smiled, "What dog, white *mon*?"

"That dog," Jack said, pointing to the shadows. The dog was gone.

"I'm out of here," Jack said, tossing the woman a twenty-dollar bill. "Here's for the hat. Keep the change."

Outside, Jack fanned at his face to chase the harsh fumes away. He crossed a small backyard overrun with debris, shooing away a half dozen chickens, pecking at the bare earth as two scrawny kittens wrestled in the dust. He sucked in the fresh air trying to clear his lungs of the smoke from the shop. Whatever that woman was smoking was potent and with each breath, he felt better. Once he was clear-headed, he peeked over the wooden fence, hoping to see some sign of Henrí. A dirty alley lined with wooden fences ran in both directions. Wooden gates broke the fence line every couple of dozen feet. Gates that led to the backyards of old clapboard houses. A loud rooster crow cut through the air from behind Jack. Startled, he swung around to see the old crone standing in the doorway pointing a gnarled finger to a house several doors down the alley. She clucked a few times and disappeared back into the shadowy shop. The wooden gate made a loud squeaking noise, as he pulled it open and stepped into the alley. The smell of rotted garbage overflowing from canisters and barrels was thick in the air. Dozens of skinny mangy dogs rutted and nosed through piles of raw garbage with their tails tucked between their bony rumps. Jack bent low, as he made his way down the alley towards the gate to which the old woman had pointed.

He stopped to listen for any sound coming from the yard or house. Slowly, he pushed the door open and peeked inside. Without any warning, a hand reached around the door, grabbed him by the head, and yanked him inside. Jack's mind went blank for a moment from the pain, as his head hit the dirt. The stitched wound on the side of his head zippered open and blood poured out over his neck, face, and chest. The man jumped back in surprise when he saw the blood-soaked Rasta hat fall to the ground, and a pale white face covered in dripping blood staring at him with blank eyes.

"*Papa Legba*! How dis happen?" The man was shocked, as he looked at all the blood and then down at his hands.

Jack rolled onto his side, tried to focus his eyes, pulled his pistol, and fired. The round went wide slamming into the fence. Within an instant, he was being lifted and carried into the kitchen of the house. Two men who were copies of the mutt in the yard dropped him on the floor. Jack reached out, grabbed a leg, and pulled, tripping one of his captors. The man was caught by surprise and reached out and grabbed his partner for support. Jack took advantage of the men being off balance, stood, and kicked the one closest to him in the crotch. The poor guy screamed in pain and fell to the floor. The other man stood frozen in fear. This was not supposed to happen. No one ever fought back against the Tonton Macoute. Was this man crazy? He watched, seemingly in slow motion, as Jack pulled a cast-iron skillet off the stove and swing it towards his head. The last thought the man had was that this was not the way it was supposed to be. The skillet slammed into the man's forehead and he dropped to the floor.

Jack was winded. He breathed in deeply, as he wiped the blood from his face with a dishtowel. He bent to pick up his pistol and came back up with vertigo. He steadied himself by leaning into the sink and pointed his pistol at a figure of a man standing in the doorway. The figure was yelling something, more like a loud croaking bark than a human yell. It was the most bizarre-looking person Jack had ever seen. It had ghostly white skin, bluish red features, and shocking yellow frizzy hair. He was dressed in a white tropical type suit with white shirt and shoes. Jack knew, instinctively, that this had to be Marcel Duvalier. The pistol wobbled in his hand as he tried to steady it on his target.

"Marcel...where's Coco? If she's hurt, I'll kill you," Jack screamed.

Without warning, the figure disappeared from the doorway. Jack heard a crash and yelling.

"Jack, Jack, in here! Hurry, he's hurting me!" Coco yelled.

"Let her go, Marcel!" Jack yelled, and fired into the floor again.

There was loud crashing and breaking of furniture, then the sound of flesh hitting flesh.

"I'll give her back to you when I am finished with her, white *mon*," Marcel croaked and laughed insanely. "Maybe you come find her in the Islands, maybe we meet there and take turns, before we cut her up. What you think, Babylon *mon*?"

Jack's vision was blurry and his head spinning, as he tried to pull himself together. He fired another warning shot into the floor and ran to the doorway and squatted. A bullet whizzed by his ear and tore a large splinter from the doorjamb. Jack's vision was still murky, but he could see several figures moving around the room. He saw a blurry white figure to his left and fired at it. A split second later, an automatic weapon fired from a different angle, spraying rounds into the wall and doorframe around Jack. The supersonic slugs sounded like angry wasps as they whizzed by him. Jack popped off a round in the direction of the automatic fire, then rolled back into the kitchen and crawled on his hands and knees out the backdoor. Once outside, he hunkered down behind a trashcan. The man who had yanked him into the yard was nowhere to be seen. The gate was jammed open and Jack ran out into the alley. He stood with his back to the fence, breathing hard, trying to clear his vision. Everything was blurry and seemed to shimmy. He slid down the fence onto his haunches, with his head in his hands, trying not to blackout. The slash on the side of his head where the stitches had separated was bleeding freely. Jack knew that head wounds always appearred to be worse than they really are, due to the amount of blood that flows. It was the blurring vision that worried him. He was in no shape to be shooting it out with a bunch of gun mutts, but he couldn't give up and let Coco be hurt. He had to get back inside and stop Marcel before he got away.

Jack made his way back into the kitchen and stood listening. The house was quiet except for a moaning sound coming from the living room. The old wood floor squeaked as he made his way into the living room, his gun at the ready. A man was slumped back on the coach holding a blood-soaked towel to his chest, bubbly gore dripped from his mouth. With each breath, the man wheezed in pain, he coughed up a gob of blood and fell back, his eyes locked on Jack.

"Help me, *mon*, I'm dying," the man whispered.

"Where's Marcel taking the woman?" Jack stood over the man with his pistol pointing at his head.

"You shot me once, now you come back to finish the job. Why you want to kill Andrew? I'm nobody." He wiped bloody froth from his mouth with the back of his hand.

Jack saw the Mac 10 machine pistol lying on the floor, "Seems this is my lucky day, Andrew. You missed on full auto and I was shooting blind. Tell me where Marcel is taking Coco and I'll get you some help."

"He's taking her to Haiti," Henrí said from a bedroom door.

Jack swung his pistol around and pointed it at Henrí, then quickly lowered it.

"Henrí, what happened? Where have you been?" Jack was relieved to see the old man and went to him.

"One of Marcel's goons bopped me in the head and knocked me out. I came to and played possum, hoping they would think I was dead. I knew you would be in to rescue me when I didn't show up at the car."

"Thank God, you're alive. They've taken Coco somewhere. I'm pushing this man for information," Jack said, as he turned to point at the man on the couch.

Jack and Henrí both stared. The man's eyes were frozen open, but he was clearly dead. His mouth hung open and lifeless. Henrí made the sign of the cross and kissed his fingers.

"His spirit is free now, no more earthly pain," Henrí said. "Jack, I heard Marcel say that he was taking Coco to Haiti and turn her over to his father, along with the information on the hidden fortune. Coco gave her mother's diary to him and told him that is the only thing that she had of her mother. If there was secret information in it, she didn't know what or where it would be. Marcel was overjoyed with the diary. He went on about how grandmamma was a clever old witch, probably had it written in code and that his father's people could decipher it." Henrí was smiling big when he said the last.

"Why are you smiling?" Jack asked.

"They can decode all day long but they won't get the information they're looking for," Henrí said, grinning. "Come with me."

Jack followed Henrí down a short hallway to a door painted with symbols of shooting stars, the moon in different phases, a crucifix with a black Jesus hung upside down, garlands of garlic, radishes, and a goatskin tacked over the frame. Henrí brushed the skin aside, pushed the door open, and motioned Jack inside. Each of the four walls had a different mural painted on it, depicting the seasons with primitive drawings of people, animals, and spirits. The ceiling was painted with stars and comets with more ghostly spirits flying across the cosmos. Jack's first thoughts were of primitive drawings made by superstitious cave dwellers. The hair on Jack's neck was standing on end.

"So, Henrí, what am I looking at here?"

"This is where I pray, this is where my Lucinda is," he said. He struck a match and lit several candles.

A table against the back wall was covered with votive candles, plates of shriveled fruit, plastic bottles of water, little bowls of animal parts, and small brass coins. A skull sat on top of a covered box in the center of the table, two fat candles, their flames fluttering deep in the melted wax, sat on either side of the skull. A pungent musty smell hung heavy in the room. Jack's eyes were watering

"Don't be afraid, Jack. This place is protected by powerful Loa spirits and many Ogua soldiers. This is my prayer room," Henrí said softly, moving across the room to the table. "Come here, and I will show you why I said the secret information is in a safe place that no one would ever touch."

Jack looked over Henrí's shoulder, confused at what he saw. The box with the skull on it was not where he had seen it a moment ago. One-half of the table was completely empty of candles, fruit, and the other offerings. Instead, he was looking at a maze of mirrors that gave the illusion of a full table but, in reality, was only half filled. The box with the head on it was even more perplexing. By some trick, the mirror reflections made the box and skull appear to rotate and move as Jack bent closer. He reached out to touch the box, but touched a mirror instead, and quickly withdrew his finger.

Henrí carefully moved two of the mirrors and the illusion disappeared. The box was sitting on the right side of the table, not even close to the center. He began to chant and sway, moving his hands and wiggling his fingers. He chanted louder. His whole body was shaking, as his hands got closer to the skull. With a quick movement, he grasped the skull in his hands, snatched it off the box, and held it aloft.

Jack shook off the feeling that something unearthly had just occurred, as he watched Henrí set the skull to the side and work a hidden catch.

"You have to be fast and catch that old man when he's not looking. You never know if he going to bark or bite."

Jack was looking closely at the ancient skull and the unusual shape of the forehead and jaw. "Is this some prehistoric skull from Africa?"

"He's from Africa, that's for sure. That's the only place I know of where baboons come from. He is an old one, too. Some say he's over five hundred years old. We don't know, for sure, how many *Bocor* have cared for him. I've had him for twenty years and when my time comes, I'll pass him on to another *Bocor* to care for him. This one is very magical and full of tricks. Don't get too close, he doesn't take to strangers."

Jack backed away from the table, keeping an eye on the ancient skull with the yellow teeth, and the other eye on what Henrí was doing. The contents of the box looked like coarse grain sand or pulverized coral. Henrí was bent over the box, sifting through it with his fingers, speaking softly and swaying his head left and right. After a few moments, he straightened and turned showing Jack a bone, or ivory tube no larger than a cigarette.

"My Lucinda has been keeping this safe all these years," he said, then turned back whispering, as he smoothed the contents out and closed the lid.

Jack stood quietly, listening to Henrí finish up with his whispered prayers. He wiped blood from the side of his face with his shirttail and winced when he touched the torn wound.

Suddenly, he felt very tired and hungry. He couldn't recall when he had eaten last, or when he had slept. Maybe it was in the hospital, but he couldn't remember. He eased back against a wall and slid down, until he was sitting on the floor, his chin settled on his chest and he slept.

"This is what Marcel is looking for..." Henrí said, as he turned and saw that Jack was snoring lightly.

Chapter 12

The room was in shadows, when Jack opened his eyes, not sure of where he was. Noise drifted in from an open window across the room, reggae music, rap, a mix of French, Creole, and English languages, screaming over each other to be heard. Car horns and clunker motors added to the cacophony of sound. The room smelled of old people, lilac sachet permeated the quilt and pillow shams. Bay rum competed with dirty socks. He guessed this was Henrí's bedroom. Another odor hung heavy in the air but he couldn't put a name to it. He didn't have any memory of how he got here, but, he was grateful for the respite. The last thing he remembered was sitting on the floor in Henrí's spirit room as the old man was bending over the makeshift altar. His headache was gone and the scalp wound had stopped throbbing.

A movement in the shadows alarmed Jack and he sat upright on his elbows. The old crone from the store came out of the shadows and stood beside the bed without a word. She craned her head in close to Jack's face and stared into his eyes, mumbled a rhyme of some sort and backed out of the room, watching Jack, as she reached behind her to open the door. She let herself out without making a sound. The nameless odor went with her. In less than a minute, the door flew open and Chief hurried in.

"Jack! Damn brother, I was worried about you. You've been out for over six hours," he said, switching on a table lamp. "I didn't know if you were unconscious from the concussion and the wound, or just worn out."

"I was just tired, I guess. I feel fine now," Jack said, he swung his legs off the bed and sat up. He was expecting a dizzy spell but was surprised when it didn't happen. "Six hours! What's happened while I was out?"

"Take it easy, we've got everything under control," Chief said, as he looked over Jack's wound. "Max is sitting in front of the Haitian Consulate building on 2nd Street, waiting to see if anything happens there. Marcel has Coco inside the consulate with him and his Tonton boys."

"No, that's the wrong place. I heard him say he was taking her to Haiti to turn her over to his father…"

"Maybe that's the plan, but as of five minutes ago, when Max checked in, Marcel was still at the consulate. That's where he went when he left here, according to Henrí's street sources. I thought it best if we let you rest for a while, since there's nothing in play, at the moment."

"Where's Henrí?" Jack stood, and balanced himself.

"He's nodding off in his rocker in the living room. The old man's in bad shape, Jack. He's popped at least five nitro pills, just in the last couple of hours. The old woman gave him some broth a while ago, and he seems to be comfortable now."

"What about the tube, the bone tube? Did he give it to you?"

"I don't know what you're talking about. What bone tube?"

Jack caught a glimpse of himself in the dresser mirror and leaned in for a closer look. The bandages from his wound were gone and the length of the wound itself was covered in a thick layer of grease. He probed the gash lightly for stitches, but couldn't find any. Someone had removed the torn stitches, and had closed the wound with salve. His fingers came away smelling of dirty socks. Whoever had worked on his wound, also, had given him a shave and put clean clothes on him. He was dressed in a pair of khaki pants and a white guayabera shirt. Jack looked at Chief questioningly.

"The old woman cleaned you up, once we moved you in here. From all the laughing and giggling coming out of this room, she was having one hell of a good time, while she was at it. She stuck her head out and said something in Creole to Henrí at one point, and they both cracked up laughing," Chief said, with a grin.

Jack found his old bloodstained clothes in a heap on the floor. He retrieved his keys and wallet and the two small bottles of painkillers and transferred it all to his new duds.

"Where's my roscoe?" he asked, as he looked around the room.

"Hell, I hope it's still between your legs. Maybe, that was what the old lady was laughing about," Chief said, with an even bigger grin.

"My pistol, Chief, I'm talking about my pistol," Jack said, shaking his head.

"Oh, that. It is on the kitchen table. I just finished giving it a good cleaning."

Jack went into the living room, saw that Henrí was sleeping, and continued into the kitchen.

"Where's the meat? The dead guy that was on the couch."

"We tossed him in the dumpster down the alley, once it got dark," Chief answered.

"We? Who's we?"

"Rooster, the old lady's son. The name doesn't fit the man, Jack. This guy is huge. He's bigger than either one of us. I think he might be a little slow in the intelligence department, but a nice fellow. Doesn't talk, always smiling."

"Have you spotted anyone watching the house?" Jack asked, as he peeked out the screen door into the darkness.

"Yeah, there's a couple of guys on each end of the block out in front, and one on each end of the alley out the back. They stick out like sore thumbs, with their sunglasses and their watermelon hats. I know they're carrying by the way they move the weight of their piece under their shirts. One of the mutts raises his shirt, so passersby can see he's carrying, showing off, I guess."

At that moment, Henrí entered the kitchen "Those men will stand there all night, without really knowing why they are there. Marcel probably told them to watch for any white men coming or going, but didn't tell them what to do if they saw them. The Tonton are ruthless and murdering bullies, but they will never take the initiative, especially, if the orders came from The Vampire himself."

"Henrí, sit down," Jack said, pulling a chair out from the small table. "Chief told me that you're having angina attacks. Do you want to go to a hospital?"

"Too much excitement the last couple of days has my heart rolling like a rollercoaster, one minute she is up, the next she is down. I'm thinking this ride is coming to an end, pretty quick, Jack. We need to get Coco back, before the Lord pulls the plug on me."

Henrí dug in his pocket, pulled out the bone, and placed it on the table. All three men stood transfixed as they looked at the small bone, yellowed with age. Jack reached out to pick it up and Henrí slapped his hand away,

"That's *gris-gris*! You don't want to touch it. No telling what kind of mischief inside that thing," Henrí said, as he inspected the cylinder. "We need to get Momma Dey back over here to handle it. She's a Voodoo *hougan* Priestess. It was her and my Lucinda that put whatever is inside that thing in there all those years ago."

"You mean you don't know what's inside that chicken leg? Here, give it to me. I'll crack it open so we can get moving," Chief said.

Henrí smacked his hand away. "Don't touch that. First off, only a Voodoo *Worker* can open a *gris-gris* that's sealed. If you try to open that, you will be cursed to kingdom come. Besides, that isn't a chicken bone."

"What do you mean? Sure looks like a leg bone to me," Chief said.

"It's a leg bone all right. It's a baby's leg bone, a very old bone. I don't think that even Momma Dey knows how old it is, but it's plenty powerful. I can feel the spirits swirling around this room watching over it."

Jack and Chief, unconsciously, looked around the room expecting to see gauzy banshees zipping around, ready to dip down and snatch their hair out with talon-sharp claws. Jack shook off the ghostly feeling and said,

"I take it that this Momma Dey is the old lady that doctored me up, right?"

"She's the one. You don't want to trifle with her, she'll throw a hex on you that will have your gut in knots for a month," Henrí laughed. "Seriously, she is one of the most powerful Voodoo *Workers* outside of Haiti. People come from all over for her advice and blessings. Most people see her coming down the street and they'll turn around and go the other way, just so none of the spirits that surround her latch on to them."

"Sounds like a lot of bullshit to me," Chief said, with a smirk.

"Ha-ha," Henrí laughed. "Chief, I'll tell her you said that."

Henrí went to the back door and opened it. "Rooster, go fetch Momma," he said softly, then closed the door.

In less than five minutes, the backdoor swung open and Momma Dey entered, carrying a covered basket and a quart whiskey bottle with a cork stopper. Rooster shut the door behind him and stood blocking it with his massive body. Jack and Chief looked at each other and both resettled their pistols in their waistbands.

Momma Dey didn't waste any time with formalities. She placed the leg bone on a swatch of black satin, then lit four votive candles and placed them on the four corners of the cloth.

Next came a chicken foot with feathers tied to it, a goat's bushy tail, several shriveled petrified lizards of different sizes, then several jars of powders and other strange items.

Without any signal, Rooster walked throughout the house turning off all the lights, then returned to his station by the door. Jack and Chief watched the proceedings closely, keeping an eye out for banshees. Both men were spooked, but would never admit it. Henrí stood in the shadows with his eyes closed. Momma Dey uncorked the whiskey bottle and filled her mouth until her cheeks were swollen, then without any warning she started spewing the whiskey out in a mist around the room. Jack tried to avoid being sprayed, but failed, and wiped his face with the sleeve of his shirt. Chief stood transfixed, his eyes wide and mouth open.

Momma Dey began to chant and sway, as she flapped her elbows. Her head rolled from side to side, her eyes were closed. Jack saw that Henrí had his arms outstretched and rolling his shoulders to the beat of the chant. His head was doing a pecking motion back and forth, while he made clucking sounds.

Rooster let out several loud bleats that made Jack flinch and duck. He eased back into the shadows. Once out of the ring of candle light, he stood with his pistol in his hand, and tried to calm his nerves, breathing through his mouth.

Momma Dey plucked her fingers into one of the jars and flicked powder over the burning candles causing them to flare up brightly. She repeated this several times. The room was heavy with smoke and the smell of sulfur. She bent forward, blew on the bone, and whispered to it. Jack watched as she bit the bone and drew it into her mouth. The room was still, no one moved, the smoke had settled to the floor. The only sound was that of Momma Dey chewing and sucking on the bone. Suddenly, Momma Dey screamed and stumbled backward away from the table. Jack jumped, and pointed his pistol at the table, not seeing anything to shoot. Chief's spell broke. He had his pistol out in a flash, and ready. He backed over to stand beside Jack,

"What the fuck!"

"Shhh," Jack said, softly.

Momma Dey sank to the floor in a faint. Rooster had slid to the floor with his back propped against the wall asleep. Henrí stood motionless with his eyes tightly closed.

No one moved for several minutes. Street sounds drifted in through the cracks and eaves of the old house, as the sulfur smoke moved out of the room on a whisper of wind. Thunder rolled off in the distance, and the pitter-patter of raindrops bouncing of the windowpanes added to the eeriness of the moment.

"Sounds like the storm is moving up this way," Jack said, to no one.

"What just happened, Jack? That was the most bizarre thing I have ever seen, and I've seen a lot," Chief said, in a whisper.

Mamma Dey stood and said something to Henrí, then walked to the table. Jack joined her. On the table, next to the bone was a tightly rolled piece of heavy paper, almost parchment, as yellow as the bone itself. Mamma Dey began to pray softly, using one finger as an anchor and unrolled the paper with another. Time and mold had eaten the uneven edges of the paper, giving it the appearance of having been burned. As it was unrolled, it crackled in the silence. Then numbers started to appear: 1…3…5…" Mamma jerked upright and stared at Henrí, in fear

"Do you see this old man?" She bent back to her work: 7….9…13

Mamma Dey crossed herself, then placed a votive candle on either side of the paper to keep it from rolling up. Jack bent in close to see better. The candle flames were flickering but there was no apparent wind. He memorized the numbers and started to straighten up. His eye caught a faded letter below the numbers. He looked closer and saw more.

"Look, Henrí, there is some writing below the numbers. Look from an angle and you can make them out."

Jack moved around the table to get a better look. Without touching the paper, he ran a fingertip above the letters attempting to make them out, "The first letter is a capital C, then…it's too faded, I can't make out the others. Wait! Here is a capital B…and a blank, then an a, and a c," Jack said.

He turned to look at Henrí who had backed away from the table into the shadows. "What's wrong?" Jack asked, puzzled.

Jack turned to see what Mamma Dey thought about the letters, but she was gone. Chief whirled around and saw that Rooster was gone as well.

"What the fuck is going on? Jack, let's get out of here! This is too fucking creepy for me," Chief said.

"I don't know, Chief, but I'm with you. This is too spooky for me, too."

Jack flipped on the kitchen light and blew out the candles on the table. As he picked up the old paper, it crumbled into small pieces and he jerked his hand back, as if he had been shocked.

"That's it, we're out of here," Chief said, as he backed away from the table.

"What happened, Jack? Did it burn you?"

"No, it just crumbled, when I picked it up. I wasn't expecting that."

Henrí bent forward, holding his chest, groaning. He fished around in his trouser pocket and pulled out a small vile of nitro tablets. He clasped the bottle between his deformed hands, twisted the cap off with his teeth, and popped a pill into his mouth. He stumbled over to the table and sat down, still clutching his heart.

Jack sat next to him, watching closely, ready to dial 911, if Henrí did not improve in a couple of minutes. Slowly, color came back in Henrí's face and his breathing was less labored.

"Jack, I need to explain. Sit here with me, until I catch my breath," Henrí said.

Chief handed Henrí a glass of ice water and sat across from Jack. He picked up Mamma Dey's basket, unceremoniously swept everything off the table into it, set it on the floor, then dusted his hands off.

"Those numbers on that piece of paper are the worst numbers in the world. Each one carries its own black magic power. If somebody wants to hurt another person in some way, they go to a Voodoo Priest or Priestess, tell them what had been done to them, and what they want done back at that person. The Priestess will check her book of numbers and then cast a spell or put a *mojo* on him, based on what the Book of Numbers says," Henrí explained.

"Momma Dey is a Priestess. So, why did she get all freaked out and disappear on us? I thought she helped Lucinda put the paper in the bone way back when. Am I wrong?"

"No, you're not wrong, but Momma Dey never saw what was on that paper. I never even knew, all these years. Only my

Lucinda knew what was written on that paper and she kept it a secret from everybody. Those numbers, when strung together the way they were, is probably the worse combination possible. Only Voodoo Priests that work in black magic would ever say those numbers aloud…"

"It's all just hocus-pocus, Henrí. You don't believe all that Hollywood make-believe stuff, do you?" Chief asked. He was still skeptical of everything he had seen and felt tonight, but there was beginning to be a kernel of doubt.

"Chief, Voodoo is like any religion. They say it is the oldest religion in the world, going back before the Garden of Eden. It has many of the same stories and beliefs that the old Bible has, even some of the same people. The difference is that the believers of Voudun, or Voodoo as most people know it, are more tuned in to the good and bad spirits that surround us and that affect our daily lives. So yes, I believe in the hocus-pocus, as you say. I will tell you that you never want to repeat this combination of numbers to any believer, unless you want to give them a heart attack."

"Where do we go from here?" Jack asked. "We have a string of black magic numbers and a few letters to work with. Not much to go on."

"You're wrong, Jack, they tell us a lot. Coco's grandmother, Madam Duvalier, was a clever old Priestess. She worked both sides of the spirit world. Sometimes, she called up the good spirits, but most times, she worked with the black side.

Most old people in Haiti believed that Madam Duvalier ran the country, and not that lazy old husband of hers. It was rumored that Papa Doc was under her spell all those years up until his death. Then she put a hex on her son, Jean Claude, Baby Doc, to do her bidding. Madam loved her daughter, Renee, very much. So, when she learned that her son, Baby Doc was jealous of Renee having a lover and was going to have her killed, it was Madam who sent a Loa spirit that made him change his mind and just banish her from the Island."

"Is this going somewhere?" Jack asked, anxious to get on the move. "Is this enough information to swap with Marcel to get Coco back?"

"I'm sure, this is what Marcel was looking for when he kidnapped Coco. When he found out that she didn't know anything, he came here and ransacked the house. He took Renee Duvalier's diary thinking that the information leading to Madam Duvalier's fortune was inside."

"But do *we* have enough information. What do these numbers tell us?"

"My guess is that the numbers are an account number. The old lady purposely used this string of numbers to scare off all except the most evil of black magic workers. No one that knows Voudun would ever pursue anything with these numbers associated with it," Henrí said.

"OK, we have us an account number, but where? Just in Miami alone there must be over a hundred banks and millions of accounts..."

"Not so fast, Jack. The next piece of the puzzle is actually easy, if you know the Duvalier's history. Madam Duvalier came from a well-off family that thought she was crazy for marrying a penniless country doctor in a penniless country. Madam ignored the pleading from her family, left her home island, and married the bumpkin. Within five years, the wedded couple were not only rich, but also high in Haiti's social circle. It is believed that Madam Duvalier made all this possible by using black magic on her husband."

"Henrí, this is a great story and needs to be written down someday, but for now, we're up against the clock..."

"Jack, give an old man his time. You need to know about history so you can see into the future, don't you see?" Henrí said, frustrated. "What I was leading up to is this..."

Henrí bent over, picked up a jar with his mangled fingers, and gave it to Chief, "Open that up and sprinkle it over the table top."

Chief shook the gritty dust contents over the table then spread it smooth with the palm of his hand.

"Jack, use your finger and write those numbers in the dust...just like you saw them."

Using his forefinger, he copied the numbers in the layer of dirt:

1 3 5 7 9 13

"OK, now, write the letters you saw, but listen to me, and I'll tell you the missing letters."

All three men bent over the table, as Jack did as he was told.

C a y B r A C

Henrí had a huge grin on his face, "There it is, Jack. *Cayman Brac,* Madam Duvalier's home Island."

"She was from the Cayman Islands?"

"Sure enough, that's where she hid all that money. Cay Brac is the littlest island in the Caymans. There isn't anything there but a prison quarry and rich folks…old Cayman rich folks. That sneaky old bitch was feeding Haiti's money back to her family, all those years. She must have set this account up for Miss Renee to see her through her life. My guess is that there's not billions stashed away as Jeanne Claude and Marcel think there is. Those billions are gone, or, so well hidden around the world that only Madam's family knows where it all is. Ms. Renee's dowry, if you want to call it that, was probably much more modest, but still big enough to see her through her life, and then some."

"But Ms. Renee, Coco's mother, drowned, so, the dowry belongs to Coco, right?" Chief asked, as things started to fall into place.

"That's the way I see it, Chief. If there is money, it belongs to Ms. Coco, all right," Henrí answered, with a grin.

"Henrí, if this is such good news for Coco," Jack said, "why did your wife hide the information from her all these years? That doesn't make sense, Coco was out working the streets to help you and Lucinda make ends meet. Why would she do this?"

Henrí was struggling to find an answer. After a few minutes of torment, he said, "Jack, the only thing that makes any sense to me is that Lucinda, after seeing those numbers, thought that it was some kind of black magic curse that Madam or Jeanne Claude had placed on Ms. Renee and that was why she drowned. I'm thinking Lucinda didn't want Coco to have that same curse put on her and that's why she hid the numbers in that baby's leg bone. Babies are innocent and can't be touched by magic. Lucinda was trying to protect Coco."

"From an outsider, that sounds ridiculous, but since I don't understand all this Voodoo stuff, I'll just have to accept your explanation," Jack said, shaking his head.

"Jack, it wasn't too long ago that women were burned for witchcraft in New England, and others were torn into parts on the rack by the Catholics, so it's not just Voodoo that has weird beliefs and practices. Every man has to look inside to determine right from wrong."

"Whoa, this is getting too deep for me. I say we go get Coco," Chief said.

Chapter 13

Max had to pee really bad. He had been holding it for several hours, as he sat watching the Haitian Consulate on 2nd Avenue, but now he needed to make an executive decision. Should he leave his post and find a restroom, or should he pee in one of the cup holders located on the center console? The parking spot directly across from the gated entry to the consulate gave him a clear view into the courtyard and both the front and side entrances to the building. If he gave up this spot to take a leak, it would be gone faster than a politician's campaign promises. On the other hand, if he peed into the cup holder, he would have to sit smelling urine for the rest of the day. He knew by the pressure on his bladder that he would easily fill both cup holders and possibly the ashtray, too. Then, there was the question of how he would empty them once the stakeout was over.

As he sat nibbling on a thumbnail trying to decide which option to take, a loud crack of thunder exploded overhead and rain poured down in sheets. The unexpected clap of thunder startled Max, causing him to almost lose control of the situation at hand. He threw up his hands, in frustration, turned his collar up, adjusted his oversized aviator sunglasses, and stepped out of the cab into the rain. He hurried over to a huge gumbo-limbo tree that had grown so big it had raised and cracked the sidewalk around it. He tripped and fell, skinning his knee on a jagged edge of concrete and tearing the fabric of his best pair of black chinos in the fall. He pulled himself up and stood facing the tree trunk, unzipping just in time, and let loose. The immediate relief was almost orgasmic, as he stood with his face tilted up and his tongue out catching the pounding rain. He involuntarily shivered when he finished and zipped up. As he turned, two fat women under a too-small umbrella were standing in front of him, slack jawed, aghast at what they had just witnessed.

"What?" Max asked, baffled by their looks.

Without a word, the two hustled off, taking turns looking back over their shoulders to see if the pervert was following them.

"Miami people are from a different universe. Don't they understand that when a man has to go, he has to go?" he thought, running back to the taxi.

"The fuck!" He pulled again on the door handle. No response, he was locked out of his own vehicle. The keys were dangling in the ignition. His cell phone was sitting in one of the cup holders, blinking, indicating a missed call.

"Jeez, now what?" He leaned against the door in thought, the rain beating down on him.

He glanced across the street and broke into a mischievous grin. *"If you can't beat 'em, join 'em."* He looked both ways for traffic and zipped across the street. As he started through the driveway gate, a uniformed security guard leaned out of an enclosure that was tucked neatly behind the compounds front wall.

"May I help you, Sir?" the guard asked, staying mostly inside the small post out of the rain.

The appearance of the guard startled Max and he slid to a stop, coming to attention. His six years as a con inside Riker's had instilled a fear of uniformed authority that was still with him, even after all these years. Anyone wearing a uniform and standing a post was automatically seen as having control of one's freedom and wasn't to be fucked with.

"Uh...yes, Sir. Simms, Max Simms...uh, permission to go inside the block...uh, the building."

"What is the purpose of your visit?"

"Uh…I was thinking about visiting Haiti. I love the Haiti people, they're like brothers to me," Max gushed, "I want to talk to someone about maybe, moving there, permanent like. I want to get a brochure or two on job availability…especially about commercial driver's licensing…"

"Excuse me sir, but are you sure you are talking about Haiti? In the Caribbean?"

"Sure. I mean, how many Haiti's are there? Of course, I'm talking about the right place," Max said, indignantly, beginning to feel more confident. "I want to talk to whoever is in charge here. Since I don't have an appointment, I'll just sit quietly inside until someone can help me…Boss."

The guard looked at Max as if he were looking at a crazy man. Who in their right mind would want to immigrate to Haiti? People were risking their lives to get off the island because of the crushing poverty, disease, and famine. Yet, here was this strange little white man wanting to go there to get a job driving a commercial vehicle. He shook his head and handed Max a laminated card with the word GUEST printed on it and the number 16.

"When they call that number, show this to the lady at the counter, she'll take care of you." The guard shook his head again, stepped back inside his post, and watched, as the wet rodent-featured little man made a broken-field dash through the rain, dodging potholes and imaginary bullets.

Inside the consulate, out of the rain, Max shook himself, like a wet birddog coming out of a pond. He removed his aviators, and with one last quick shake and took in his surroundings. In spite of the storm, the greeting hall was filled with people, each with a numbered card in hand, all sitting on benches that ran across the waiting room, five rows deep. Max took a seat at the end of the backbench, and hunched over to appear smaller than he was, just as he had done as a kid when he went into St. Patty's in Manhattan to swipe money out of the offering box. In his mind, this was his non-threatening posture and most people tended to ignore him after an initial glance. From his vantage point, he scoped out the room and knew instantly from a loser lifetime of line waiting, it would be a long wait. He spotted the restroom sign and headed for it. The MEN's room was down a narrow hall on the left, out of sight of the waiting room. Max noted that there was a door at the end of the hall and another across from the restroom. He ducked into the restroom and quickly secured a toilet, sliding the bolt closed behind him. He dropped his pants, sat, and began pulling toilet paper off the roll to dry himself. Satisfied that he was as dry as he could be using tissue, he sat thinking, chewing his pinky nail painfully to the quick. He knew Coco was in this building somewhere with Marcel, the Midget. He thought of the Tonton leader as shorter than himself, and therefore, an easy target to vent on. Without an exact plan, he envisioned rescuing Coco through force of arms against the midget and becoming the hero de jour. He was brought back to the present by a loud explosion of gas from the stall next to his that brought him to his feet. He quickly zipped, buckled up, and left the stall. Another explosion made him gasp.

"Hey, how about a courtesy flush in there? A man can't breathe with that going on. Jeez!"

Max washed his hands, wiped them dry with paper towels, and left the restroom. Rather than turning right to the waiting room, he turned left and pushed through the closed door. He was in an interior hallway with doors on either side every fifteen feet or so. His beating heart was the only sound in the carpeted hallway, as he tried to control the urge to soil himself. Max knew from experience that when his body suddenly developed the urge to void itself that he was in for trouble. He wanted to turn and run as fast as he could back to the men's room, but was too frightened to turn around. Fear that some hoodoo guy was right behind him that would turn him into a zombie, propelled him forward.

The hallway made a T-intersection. Without thinking why, he took the right hallway and quickened his step. A door to his right swung open as he passed it.

He screamed, sucked in air, and screamed louder. The midget was standing there, not two feet away, with eyes bulging and frogmouth gaping, as surprised as Max was. Marcel screamed and slammed the door in Max's face. Max was terrified of the aberration he had just seen, *"What the fuck was that?"* Marcel pulled the door open a crack and peeked out. Empty, the hallway was empty.

Chapter 14

Jack stood, huddled under a small bodega's overhang across the street, fifty meters from the Haitian Consulate entrance. The thin poncho he had bought at Mama Dey's herbal shop was keeping him dry from the knees up. The hood was too small and was pushed back off his head. A Miami Dolphins cap hid his eyes in shadows, as he studied the entrance to the consulate. Rooster was standing off to the side of the bodega in the shadows. His yellow rain slicker was shiny as the lights from passing cars reflected off the wet material. His black face, hands, and feet absorbed the light and gave the impression that the raingear was suspended in midair. Momma Dey had given Rooster instructions to stick close to Jack and do everything he said. Without a word, Rooster stepped close to Jack in his Mother's small shop and ran his two hands down Jack's face, feeling every curve and contour, then bent forward and sniffed around his ears and mouth. Jack stood motionless, with only his eyes following the giant man-child's moves. With a grunt, Rooster stepped back satisfied that he had Jack's scent burned into his sensory bank.

Rain was falling, but not as heavy as a few hours ago. The hurricane seemed to slacken off, as they usually do when stalled over land for a while. With any luck, it would downgrade to a tropical storm, and blow through overnight. Jack was tired and ached from all the action the last twenty-four hours, but shook it off. He was determined to get Coco out of the consulate building, even if he had to shoot his way in and out again. Jack had been protective of Coco from the first night he met her standing inside the Sand Bar. He felt an immediate bond with her that he could never explain or even tried to understand. Coco was…Coco, and he was her protector. Since that time, she and Jack had grown closer, each feeling the bond of friendship grow into a deep familial love. They were family.

Chief and Henrí were in the shadows on the opposite end of the block from the consulate entrance. Chief had already jimmied Max's car door open and retrieved his cell phone and the ignition keys. He locked the door behind him and joined Henrí behind the giant Gumbo-Limbo tree.

"Let's just hang here until Jack calls with a plan," Chief said, as he huddled under his raingear.

"Nah, smells like peepee here, let's move down to the corner," Henrí said, in shallow breaths.

"Your heart hurting you?"

"Uh-uh, smells like somebody ate a bunch of bad papaya's and passed 'em under this tree."

Chief took a deep sniff and gagged, "Let's move it."

Jack checked the time on his watch and decided that there was not any reason to drag this out. He guessed that somehow Max had gotten himself spotted and was either dead, or being held inside the consulate, otherwise, he would have called or been in touch by now. An earlier stroll past the drive entrance gave Jack a good idea of the compound's layout, in the front and sides, as well as, the guardhouse location. The building appeared to be closed for the night, with only a few dim interior lights showing. The heavy rain was keeping the guard inside warm and dry. A portable radio was set on a Bahamas station playing reggae. No problem from that quarter.

Jack hit Chief's speed dial number on his cell phone.

"Yeah?"

"Rooster and I are going over the sidewall in two minutes. Have Henrí sit in the cab ready for a signal to drive into the compound, and pick us up on the fly," Jack said.

"What about me?"

"Stand on the street side of the compound's entrance. If the guard comes out of his shack and looks like he is alarmed and heading for the main building...stop him."

"Roger that," Chief answered, and hung up.

Jack motioned for Rooster to follow him, as he cut away from the bodega and started for the compound. He approached the wall of a dry cleaner's shop next-door. He followed the wall back almost to the rear wall and stopped. Jack guessed the wall to be around ten feet high, with broken glass shards cemented into the top blocks as a cheap security deterrent to keep someone from hopping over the wall. Jack went back up the walkway and picked up a brick he had spotted a few moments ago, and returned to the spot where he was going over the wall. He motioned Rooster to lean forward with his hands braced on the wall and his feet shoulder-width apart. This placed Rooster at almost a 45° angle to the wall and made a perfect ladder. Without any hesitation, Jack placed one foot behind Rooster's calf, and climbed forward placing his other foot on his buttocks. Then, he pulled up and placed a foot on Rooster's shoulder and grabbed the top of the wall with one hand to steady himself, and started knocking the glass shards off with the brick. Satisfied that he wouldn't cut himself, he pulled himself up and over the top, dropping into the compound's side driveway. He whirled around, drawing his pistol from his waistband at the soft touch on his shoulder. Rooster had taken off his yellow slicker, pulled himself up and over the wall, dropped to his feet next to Jack and was almost invisible in the shadows. His jeans and black t-shirt were wet and clinging to his skin. The only indication a man was standing in front of Jack were the two white round eyes.

"Damn, Rooster, don't do that. I almost capped you, dude."

Without waiting for a response, Jack trotted towards the back of the building. Several cars were parked against the wall next to a large trash incinerator that was being fed large bags of trash by a man dressed in sports jacket and slacks. Jack watched, as the man stuffed a heavy bag into the fire and slammed the door closed. The man hunched his shoulders against the rain and ran for the backdoor. Jack's curiosity got the best of him, wondering why someone would bother with trash during a downpour. He trotted over to the furnace, swung opened the cast iron door, and immediately slammed it shut. The smell of burnt flesh and singed hair gagged him. He bent at the waist and threw up. He snapped upright. *Coco!* He yanked the door back open, holding his breath, grabbed a handful of something malleable and pulled. He yelled, as the scorched head and upper torso of a man cleared the opening and fell forward to the pavement, the feet dangling up in the air. Jack backpedaled to get away from the dead man, bumped into Rooster, and tripped.

Jack held his hand over his nose and mouth and crab-crawled back to the torso, maddened with the thought that if it wasn't Coco, was it Max? He grabbed a piece of fabric and twisted. The torso flopped over and Jack let out a sigh of relief...it wasn't Max.

"Thank God," Jack moaned, just as Rooster scooped him up over his shoulder and ducked behind one of the parked cars. Two men came out of the backdoor, laughing and talking loudly, jumped into a paneled van, cranked it up, and sped out of the lot.

"Thanks Rooster, I didn't hear anything. I guess I was too excited about the body and all," Jack said.

"Rooster don't like bad men. Bad men hurt Rooster."

Jack's head snapped around, totally caught off guard by hearing Rooster speak. He just assumed that Rooster was mute and now to hear him speak made him smile and happy for him.

"Rooster, you can talk," Jack said, as he reached up and clapped him on the shoulder.

Rooster's response was a big grin. A noise caught his attention and he pushed Jack down to the deck. He peeked over the trunk of the car they were behind and moaned softly. Jack fought free of Rooster's grip, and crouched next him. A man's head was sticking out the back door looking right and left. Satisfied the coast was clear, he emerged and stood under the overhead light, looking around and snapping his fingers nervously. He started to his left, paused, whirled around, and started right.

"Pssst, Max, over here," Jack stage-whispered, as he recognized the jerky movements of his friend.

"Jackie, is that you?" Max whispered back, bending forward peering into the shadows.

"Yeah, get over here, pronto, before someone else comes out that door."

Max ran a zigzag pattern through the rain, sliding in behind the car, crashing into Rooster.

"*The fuck*!" Max said, jumping back. "What's with Dumbo being here? We expecting a zombie attack, or something?"

"Shhh, quiet down, Max. He's here to help." Jack said, as he pulled Max close to him. "Am I glad to see you, buddy! I was worried to death about you. Did you see Coco…what's going on inside…can we get her out?" Jack blurted.

"Did you really worry about me, Jack, ya swear?" Max asked, with a catch in his throat. "You would have been proud of me, Jack. I've been ducking in and out of offices and restrooms for the last three hours. I came face to face with the midget one time, but just as I was reaching out to strangle him, he slammed the door in my face…chickenshit bastard."

"Slow down and tell me what you saw…"

"I saw Coco, but you don't want to know what they were doing to her, Jack. It was awful. They have her down in a kind of basement place, more like a bunker or a crash room for a bunch of guys. The midget stood to one side, watching as some of his boys slapped Coco around, knocking her around and giving her a few kicks. It made my blood boil, just watching. I was just about to crash in on them with my straight razor out and swinging when I had to duck back into the hall broom closet. Somebody was hurrying down the steps." Max paused long enough to suck in a chest full of air. "…I heard 'em talking loud about some kind of coded message…and, that it was still missing…and that the bitch lied to them. I snuck back across the hall, just in time to see the midget's people tying Coco to a chair. At that point, I decided I better get out of there and get some help."

Jack put his arm around Max's shoulders, "You did good, Pal."

"Is that what I think it is over there?" Max said, pointing to the smoldering body a few feet away.

"It is. One of Marcel's guys was stuffing him into the opening when I came around the corner. I don't have a clue who it is, and don't care at this point."

Jack flipped his cell phone open and hit Chief's speed dial number.

"Yeah?" Chief answered, on the first ring.

"Change in plans. Take the guard out and hotfoot it to the rear of the building. You'll be passing Max on the way, do not shoot him. Do it now." Jack said, and flipped the cell closed.

"Max, this is important. On my signal, haul ass down the drive and out the front gate. Don't worry about the guard, just run as fast as you can. Tell Henrí to stand guard under that big gumbo-limbo tree. Bring your taxi around to the back door, have the doors open, and the motor running. When we come out of that door, we'll be moving fast, so, you be ready to roll. Got it?"

"Sure, Jackie, whatever you say. What if somebody else comes out first?"

"You still have your pop gun under the front seat?"

"Yeah."

"Use it."

Chapter 15

Coco held her eyes closed tight and fought her bonds, as Marcel stood, bent in front of her with his face just inches away. Coco gagged at the stench of Marcel's fetid breath on her face, as she struggled to pull away. She couldn't stand to look into his blue eyes, sunken into those red-rimmed sockets. His orange wiry hair against the bluish-white skin sent chills down her spine.

"My lovely Cousin, you lied to me. You didn't tell me the truth about your mother's journal. We didn't find anything regarding the treasure that your traitorous grandmother stole from our grandfather," Marcel croaked. "I am very close to turning you over to my Tonton soldiers to play with, my pretty," he threatened. "My father needs that treasure returned. He needs it to regain the presidency so that the Duvaliers can rule the country again. Without those funds, we will not achieve our goal…and you, a common street whore, are the only thing standing between success and us. My father is waiting, anxiously, for the good news of its return, Cousin."

"You're not listening to me Marcel. I don't know anything about any treasure. Do you think I would have lived the way I did if I had money? Do you think I liked what I had to do to survive? You little worm, I'll tell you this. Even if I knew where my mother hid the secret, I wouldn't tell you. I'll go to my grave before I would help you and that freak family of yours," she said, spitting each word out. "Oh yes, I know all about you Duvaliers and your insane lust for power. I know how our family killed and destroyed thousands of our people, so that you could live up in the mountains in your villas and your lavish life styles, while our people starved eating mud and grass...during the good years, and then, eating each other in the bad years."

Marcel tossed his head back and laughed a maniacal cackle. His flunkies joined in the laughter, anticipating the signal from their master turning them loose to rape and torment this beautiful woman. Knowing from past experience how much their boss enjoyed watching them brutalize and ultimately kill their victim, they were anxious to get started.

Without any warning, Marcel smashed his fist into Coco's face, then immediately jumped back shaking and holding his fist painfully,

"Oh, oh, I broke my hand, you filthy bitch," he screamed, as he tried to shake the pain away.

Coco was unconscious, with her chin resting on her chest, blood drooling out of her broken mouth into her lap.

Marcel was hopping around in circles sucking on his fingers and crying in pain. After a few moments, he regained control and stood shaking, his face a mask of hate and insanity.

His men watched in fear, not knowing what their master was going to do. They knew to keep their mouths shut, for fear of being the target of his wrath.

"Untie her and spread her out on the table here. We're going to see if she likes the taste of her own flesh," Marcel croaked, as he ripped off his bloodstained jacket and rolled his sleeves up.

The four men rushed to obey their master, cutting and ripping at Coco's bonds and clothes. Cut free, she tumbled to the floor. This angered one of the men and he started kicking her in the ribs. Suddenly, a small hole appeared in the man's forehead, and a misty red spray blossomed out behind his head. The man dropped to the floor, dead.

The noise from the shot froze everyone in place, they watched in slow motion as the red bloom of the man's brains painted the far wall. In an instant, every head swung back to the door, eyes bulging, mouths gaping in surprise and alarm. Two white men, with pistols aimed at them, stood at each side of the door. A giant black man stood in the doorway, a lug wrench in one hand, the other was extended out to his front, huge pink palm with an eye tattooed in its center with wiggly lines extending out to all the major compass points. Instant recognition of the Voodoo spirit world's death eye symbol made the men gasp.

All eyes were focused on the pink palm Voodoo tatoo. Time stood still, the fear palpable. Then, the spell broke. Marcel jumped back behind the closest man to him,

"Kill the whites! They are from Babylon, here to enslave us!" He screamed.

Two of the men fumbled for their weapons. Jack shot the closest one to him, watched, as he was thrown back by the impact, and then took aim at the second one. As he began to squeeze the trigger, something whistled past his head. The man screamed and fell backwards with the blade of the lug wrench buried in his chest.

Marcel's human shield fainted, as Chief rushed him. Chief grabbed the limp body by the throat and shook it like a terrier. Satisfied that the man wasn't going anywhere, he knelt over the man Jack had shot. The man was gasping for air, blood bubbled out of the hole in his chest. It was just a matter of minutes and the man would be dead.

Rooster took two giant steps, placed a hand on each side of Marcel's head, and picked him up, letting his feet dangle and kick in midair.

"Mister, you a bad boy. You hurt Ms. Coco. Now Rooster hurt you back...," he said, as Marcel grasped the big hands that had begun to squeeze and fought against the mounting pressure.

"Rooster, drop him!" Jack yelled. "I want him alive."

Without any hesitation, Rooster let go of his death grip on Marcel's head and stepped back. Marcel hit the floor, sprang to his feet, and darted for the door. As quick as a mongoose, he was gone.

"Halt!" Chief yelled, running to the door.

A jagged splinter from the doorjamb tore into Chief's forearm as he cleared the door, then ducked when a second shot zipped inches from his head. Chief stuck his arm around the corner and cranked off three fast shots up the hall. A wild laughing cackle bounced back and then a door slammed

Jack propped Coco up and brushed the blood-matted hair out of her face while he inspected her injuries. He wiped the blood from the cut on her cheek and split lips. Her two eyes were swollen shut. A front tooth was missing and her nose was a flattened mess.

"Coco, honey, can you hear me?" Jack said, softly. "I've got you, you're safe. Now, just hang on, until we get you out of here."

"Jack, Marcel is gone. You want me to go after him?"

"No, let's get the hell out of here before someone decides to see what all the shooting is about. We'll even up with Marcel later."

Chapter 16

Max hunkered down behind the incinerator, peeking around the corner, expecting trouble at any second. He was panting hard, breathing through his mouth rapidly, out of fear and excitement. When the shooting inside started, he had been sitting in his cab with all the doors wide open, motor running, and pistol in hand, as Jack had instructed. Unconsciously, he sat twirling the small .22 Berretta on his finger, old west style, forward a few flips, backwards a few flips.

When the first shot echoed out the back door, Max was up and out of his cab, running for cover. He felt disgusted with himself for hiding, but, quickly, convinced himself that it was a case of survival of the fittest. Besides, he had a better chance of bushwhacking any bad guys from this position. A couple of minutes, slowly, passed, then a burst of gunfire rolled out of the building. Max flipped his pistol faster, faint from lack of oxygen. It went quiet. Just a heavy mist falling, making the area spooky. Goose bumps ran a marathon up and down his neck. He inched out from his hiding place and shivered, as he tiptoed past the charred body. He made it to the center of the driveway and stopped. The pounding of running feet echoed off the walls. A moment of panic froze him in place. He wanted to vomit, his sphincter was a second away from complete overload…and collapse.

Marcel was running hard, looking back over his shoulder, when he made it to the parking area out in back. Just when he thought he had made good his escape, he smashed into a figure standing right in his path. The two men fell to the ground tangled in flailing arms and legs. Both men screamed and cried out in surprise. Max was terrified striking out blindly with fists and feet. Marcel fought back just as violently. Neither of the men had the power to do much damage to the other, but, for anyone looking on, it would have appeared like a battle to the death with all the squeals, grunts, and screams. Suddenly, a pistol shot rang out and the two men froze in mid-struggle, looking into each other's terrified eyes, each doing a quick inventory to see where he had been shot.

Max blinked and groaned. He fell away and collapsed onto his back, pulling his right leg up to his chest. Blood was soaking his chinos below the knee.

He cried out in pain, "Ya bastard, ya killed me…," Max fainted, and fell back to the pavement, his eyes open, but unseeing.

Marcel didn't waste a second. He untangled himself from the knot of arms and legs. Before he turned to make good his escape, he reached down and pried the small pistol out of the other man's hand. The dumb bastard had shot himself in the calf. Marcel tossed the pistol into the incinerator, and then struggled with Andre's scorched body to get *it* back into the incinerator. "This should have been burned yesterday. Why do I always have to do the dirty work? Someone will pay dearly for this," he mumbled, as he slammed the cast-iron door and brushed his hands. A minute later, Marcel was behind the wheel of his car, tearing out of the compound on to Second Avenue and safety. He had to get away and think of what his next moves would be to get the account information. His father did not abide failure, but, more importantly, he wanted to find and kill the men that had just ruined his evening of torture and pleasure with his cousin. Marcel whipped his Mercedes up onto I-95, heading south for his villa on Key Biscayne. The tropical villa was a *gift* from a fat mulatto and his pale wife before they disappeared for reneging on a promise of a large contribution to his father's presidential campaign.

Chapter 17

Jack crashed out of the back door, slamming it hard against its stops. Rooster had Coco in his arms, wrapped in a blanket, and Chief acted as tail end, Charlie covering their six. The group pulled up short and took in the empty cab, motor still running, doors open, but no Max.

"Max," Jack called out.

"Jackie, over here! I've been shot!" Max yelled back.

Jack ran to the sound of Max's voice and spotted him sitting up, grasping his leg in pain.

"Jackie, the son of a bitch shot me. I had the best of him, going toe-to-toe, I gave him a half dozen hard shots to the midsection, the punk was mine. He body slams me, just as I was going in for the coup de grâce, pulls in close, and shoots me. The son of a bitch. I go down for the count and when I come to, he's gone."

"Take it easy. Let's get you into the cab and I'll take a look at your wound," Jack said, as he helped Max up.

Max skipped one-legged to the cab, moaning and grunting.

"I don't think I'm going to make it, Jack. I think I'm bleeding out. I'm a little guy and don't have as much of the red stuff as bigger men have. Maybe you should drop me off at Jackson, the doctors are all Cuban and can't speak English, but it's free," Max groaned.

Jack ripped the chino pant leg up to Max's thigh to inspect the wound up close.

"Max, this is your lucky day," Jack said, sitting back. "You have a hole in the front of your calf and an exit hole out the back, no bleeding…"

"What! Let me see that," he sat up and took a close look. "The son of a bitch winged me. Two to one says the fucking bullet was dipped in some kind of Voodoo shit."

"Jack, we best be moving. There's a crowd growing out front, and not just looky-loos, neither," Henrí called out, hurrying around the building's corner.

Chapter 18

It was quiet in the cab, on the ride back to Key West. Jack was behind the wheel, fighting the Mother of all headaches as he winced with each oncoming headlight. An icicle of pain pierced his right eye with every passing high beam. Chief was riding shotgun, snoring softly, his chin resting on his chest. Coco was curled up with her head in Rooster's lap sleeping peacefully as Rooster hummed and clucked to her. A tired Henrí sat upright, politely listening to Max tell about his scuffle with Marcel, and how next time he got his hands around the midget's throat, it was going to be all over for the mutt.

The miles breezed by, as they blew through Key Largo, then Islamorada, Marathon, and over the seven-mile bridge. Highway 1 was dark and wet from all the rain that had fallen over the Keys the last couple of days. The shoulders of the highway were littered with coconuts, palm fronds, and little night critters scurrying around. The rain had stopped and the wind had died down, but the cloud cover remained. Jack thought it strange for the storm to just stop in place like this. Maybe it was the eye, and it was building up for a second blow.

It was after three in the morning when Jack pulled the cab over to the curb in front of Dr. Laura Summers's old refurbished conch house on Angela Street. Like all houses in Key West, Dr. Summers's two-story hundred-year-old place sat almost flush with the sidewalk. A small strip of flowerbed separated the walkway from a step up covered wood porch that ran the length of the house. Several rockers and wicker chairs lined each side of the front double doors and baskets of bougainvillea and tropical succulents hung from the overhead, casting the porch into dark shadows.

A dimmed light sat on a small table in the foyer, the rest of the house was shadows within shadows. Jack rang the doorbell and waited. A few moments later, he hit it again and held it down. His charges spread out and flopped down on the porch chairs. All of them were hurt, tired, sore, and beaten down from all the danger and excitement of the last thirty-six hours. Jack had decided on coming to Dr. Summers house rather than the Keys Hospital, mainly because of the questions and trouble they would have, regarding the types of wounds and injuries that needed treating had they gone to the emergency room. He was not ready to answer those questions yet, and, especially, if Chief Taylor stuck his nose into it. Dr. Summers was the only person he felt they could trust for now, even though he had never met her until the other night when she had worked on his concussion. The other reason, and probably the true reason, was that he was attracted to her and thought she had felt the same. Jack knew he was a dunce, when it came to matters of the heart and usually confused lust with love. It amazed him that he was even capable of thinking about love or sex, at this moment, as bad as he felt, but here he was.

A light came on at the head of the stairs and the blurry silhouette of Dr. Summers could be seen through the thick mosaic door glass. She was tightening a robe around her waist as she hurried down the stairs.

"OK, OK, coming, coming," she called out, trying to see who it was through the heavy glass.

She opened the door a few inches and recognized Jack,

"Mr. Marsh, what are you doing here?" she asked, with a mix of surprise and concern looking at the man standing in front of her. His clothes were dirty and blood stained, he was haggard and unshaven, and had a pistol stuck in his waistband.

"Are you ok?"

"We need help," he said, as he pushed passed her.

She jumped back when a huge black man, carrying an unconscious woman wrapped in a blanket, entered on the heels of Jack. Then, another big man, with a shaved head, and a bloody tourniquet on his upper arm, winked at her, as he brushed by. Behind him was another black man that appeared to be well into his nineties and had a thick bottle glass lens on one side of the frame and a solid colored lens on the other. He smiled, as he passed her, exposing gums where his top and bottom teeth should have been.

"Evening Ma'am. Sorry for the intrusion at this late hour," he said, touching a gnarled and tortured hand to his forehead in salutation.

"Good evening," was all she could answer.

She watched them parade into her house and come to a stop at the base of the stairwell.

"Are there more of you?"

"Yeah, I'm coming," Max called out from the porch. "I don't like this Jackie, you know what that is across the street, don't you?"

"Max, give it a rest. Yes, I know what *that* is. It's the Key West Cemetery. Now, come in and shut the door," Jack said, tired of Max's constant complaining and looking for trouble.

"Cemetery, my ass. Sure, maybe a hundred years ago, it could be called that, a place where decent people were laid to rest. Now, it's a frigging dumping ground for anybody that turns up dead by murder, or any other lethal means not permitted by law. It's a frigging boneyard."

"Come in, and close the door, Max. We have more to worry about than how someone might end up across the street."

"What are you doing, Mr. Marsh? Who are these people and why are you here?"

"You're a doctor, aren't you? You have an office or clinic here, right? We need to have Coco checked out, like, right now…"

"Hold on. I'm not checking anyone out, until you tell me what is going on here." Dr. Summers jutted out her chin as she spoke. "Do I need to call the police?"

"Listen, Doc, the *last* thing we need right now is the police. This party's not over yet, so, we don't need the Key West cops running around with six shooters popping," Jack said, exhausted from the night's efforts. "As for who these people are, that is Coco Duvalier. She was kidnapped, beaten, raped, and held as a prisoner, until we rescued her. The bald guy is Chief Drummond. He has a wood splinter the size of a two-by-four stuck in his shoulder, and needs to get it out before it takes root and sprouts leaves. Max Simms, you know already. He has a gunshot wound in the leg and has lost a lot of blood. I think he is suffering from shock and should probably be given a shot of something to quiet him down."

"Hey, what are ya saying? I don't need any shot. Maybe I'll give you a shot across the lips…"

"See what I mean, Doc? The sooner the better."

Jack pointed to Rooster. "The fellow standing there is a little behind on current events, but dependable. He's one of the team after tonight's work. The man knows his way around a tire tool." Jack said, affectionately. "The old guy is Coco's Uncle Henrí. He has more scars than a Florida Bay manatee, a man of few words, but a million years of wisdom."

"And you, Mr. Marsh? What is ailing you, brain damage from the concussion?" Dr. Summers folded her arms across her chest, as she spoke.

Jack sighed. "Look Doc, we need your help. We're hurt and beat up, and need somewhere safe, somewhere where we can catch our breath before round two starts. I thought we would be safe here with you, but maybe I was wrong," Jack said, as he pushed off the wall. "Let's go people, I made a mistake, there's no help here…"

The group groaned and turned to shuffle out.

"Hold it." Dr. Summers held up her hands. "Stop. Everyone just stop! I did not say I would not help. I just wanted to know what was going on. It's almost four in the morning. I'm not used to having patients show up at this hour." She brushed hair from her face, tugged on her robe, and pointed to Rooster. "You, big boy, bring the woman in here. Mr. Simms, sit down and get the weight off that leg. Chief Drummond, come with me. Mr. Marsh, you and uncle what-ever, go to the kitchen and put a pot of coffee on…a big pot," she said, hustling around Rooster to lead the way to her small clinic.

Chapter 19

Chief Drummond sat on a dock bench massaging his shoulder lightly, while he waited for the harbor taxi to return from its rounds out along the anchorage line. He needed to get out to the *Island Queen* to make sure that she had ridden out the storm okay, and then, to bring her back to her dockside mooring. Doc Summers had pulled a large splinter from the fleshy part of his upper arm and stitched it up with neat precise knots. Drummond took the digging and stitching without a wince, but when Dr. Summers hit him with an antibiotic injection, he let out a yell.

"Damn, Doc! Take it easy," he had yelled.

"Oh, you big baby, where is that macho swabbie grit you sailors are famous for? Suck it up, big boy," Doc Summers smirked, jokingly.

It was just a little past seven and the sun was trying to cut through the remaining clouds lingering over Old Town. Chief watched as gulls flitted about, diving into the flotsam that the storm had blown in around the wharf. A brown pelican sat, just out of reach, watching Chief suspiciously, plopping its long beak as a warning not to screw with it. Chief waited for his chance and flipped a gum wrapper at the bird. The bird caught the wrapper in its beak, squawked loudly, and charged. Caught by surprise, Chief threw his hands up to protect his head and ducked down. The pelican rose into the air as it made a running take off, one wingtip hit Chief, then he was airborne and flying off over the harbor.

"Ya stupid bird! Ya scared the squat out of me," Chief yelled after it.

"That'll teach you to mess with Mother Nature."

Chief swung around at the sound of the voice and shaded his eyes to see who it was. He recognized the green khaki uniform of a sheriff's deputy, and sat back. This deputy was as big as Rooster and just as black. A wicked pink scar ran down one side of the man's face, ending at the corner of his mouth, making him appear to be sneering. His eyes were narrow and hate- filled. Chief's radar was sending out alarm signals and his mind was spinning cover stories for everything he had ever done…especially in the last forty-eight hours.

"Top of the morn, Deputy."

"Whatever," the man said, taking up a position in front of the Chief, hands on hips, feet spread, and leaning forward.

"Alfred Drummond?" the man asked. "Are you Alfred Drummond?"

"Yeah, but no one has called me Alfred since I was a boot seaman. I'm Bull Drummond, Chief Bull

Drummond, late of the United States Navy. What can I do for you?" Chief said, as he stuck out his hand.

The deputy ignored the proffered hand, and said, "You work for Jack Marsh?"

"Yeah, I'm the skipper of his salvage business and his boat, the *Island Queen*. What's with the questions?"

"Where's your boss?" The deputy was rocking back and forth on his spit-shined brogan lace ups. "The sheriff needs to speak to him about a kidnapping and shooting that Marsh was involved in the other night. I'm looking for him with a summons forthwith from the sheriff."

"A forthwith? What is that, some kind of new P.C. code for a bogus jam up?"

"Watch it, wiseass. We know all about you and that terrorist crap you pulled when you worked for the TSA over at the Keys International. Not real smart. Even for a swabbie, it was dumb," the deputy said, with a sneer, clearly trying to provoke Chief.

Chief had always been slow to anger…well, somewhat slow, but when he did get angry, it, usually, ended badly for him. He took several deep breaths.

"I'm not looking for trouble, Deputy. I don't know where Marsh is, and if I did know, I would tell you."

"Well, we know he's not out there on the *Island Queen*. That was the first place we looked, and I mean we tore that boat up looking for him, every square inch and not a sign of him..."

"You were on the *Queen*?" Chief said, low in his throat as he stood, balling his fists.

"Yeah, early this morning, when we got a BOLO from the Miami PD about a carload of punks that shot up the Haitian Consulate, then made off in a hot-pink taxi. Dumb butts, there's only one hot-pink taxi in the world, and it's owned by one of your boss's flunkies"

"Never mind that, tell me what you did to the *Queen*," Chief demanded, as he moved within inches of the deputy's face. "That's private property. It's also against maritime law to board any vessel without permission..."

"Back off, sailor boy. We're the law in this town, and we go and do, as we please. We have reason to believe that Jack Marsh was involved in the murder of two Haitian nationals last night in that shoot out in Miami. That gives us all the right we need."

"Murder! Jack Marsh a murderer? I don't think so. You people are hunting the wrong dog, Deputy. Marsh is an upstanding businessman in town, as well as, involved in the community. Nah, you guys have it wrong."

"Step back, you're in my space," the deputy said, leaning forward so that his nose was almost touching Chief's.

Chief knew he was seconds away from going to jail, if he did what he wanted to do. He wanted to snap this guy's neck, toss him in the harbor, and let the gulls pick at his bones. But common sense prevailed, and he backed off.

"Sorry, Officer. You're right, I have bad eyes and can't judge distances. It's the reason I left the Navy," Chief weaseled. He would be more valuable to Jack on the outside than the inside, so eating a little crow wouldn't kill him. "I don't know where Jack is, but if I see him, I'll sure tell him that the sheriff wants to talk to him…forthwith."

The deputy was taken aback at the sudden change in Chief's attitude, and seemed to be caught off guard. "No, don't tell him that. Tell him that Deputy Coltier needs to speak to him regarding the B&E of the Haitian Consulate in Miami, as well as, the kidnapping of his employee, Coco Duvalier, the other night, and her subsequent rescue attempt," he said, handing Chief a business card.

"No problem. I can do that, Deputy. I don't know when I'll see him, but, you can trust me to tell him that he must get in touch with you."

"That's better, Mr. Drummond." The deputy stood to his full height and hooked his thumbs in his pistol belt. "They said that you're a straight shooter, Chief. I can see why. You seem to be a man who is willing to work with another person for the right reasons…if there are rewards and future opportunities in it for you. Am I right?"

Chief's mind was gonging ship's alarms…*Dive, Dive, Dive,* as he leaned forward, pretending to not quite understand.

"I'm always open to opportunity. What do you have in mind, Deputy Coltier?"

"That's what I thought. Let's say, you help me find Marsh, and I'll see that you get a nice *reward* for your effort," he said, smiling wickedly and squinted his eyes. "Once he's out of the way, maybe you can lead me to his friend, Coco Duvalier."

"Coco! You want to meet Coco? Hell, that's no problem. If she turns up, I'll introduce you to her. No big deal."

"Chief, don't be thick headed. I don't want to be introduced to her. I want her for…a friend of mine. My friend greatly admires her and wants to spend time with her. Do you catch my meaning?"

"Yeah, I guess so. I'd kind of like a little of that myself," Chief said, with a wink.

"Trust me, you won't want any of it once my friend finishes with her," the deputy laughed, exposing a gold tooth where the right canine tooth should have been. The point of the tooth had a pointed blood-red ruby imbedded in it.

Chief cocked his head, as he looked closer at the tooth, "Is that a stone mounted on the tip of that tooth? I've never seen anything like that before. Looks like a …"

"Never mind, that's none of your business," Deputy Coltier snapped. "Just keep your mind on the job."

Deputy Coltier tipped his head, turned, walked back to his patrol unit, and drove off. Chief watched the supercharged unit cut across the crushed coral lot, hitting water-filled potholes, as it picked up speed. He sneered. It was obvious to him that Coltier was tied in with Marcel Duvalier somehow, maybe on his payroll or maybe just a freelancer out to make a score. Either way, he needed to get hold of Jack and give him a heads up.

Chapter 20

Jack's tongue and throat were raw from all the coffee he had consumed. His eyes burned from lack of sleep, and his cheeks and chin itched from the three-day stubby growth. The news from Chief Drummond that one of Sheriff Taylor's deputies might be tied, somehow, to Marcel, and was hunting him and Coco had him, gravely, worried. Jack knew that what he had done at the consulate was justified, from a *correct thing to do* standpoint, but, as for the law, that was different. He had hoped that Marcel would tuck tail and back off, since he had started the mess. This whole nightmare never would have happened, if Marcel and his men had not abducted, raped, and tortured Coco, to find the key to some supposed fortune.

Jack was tempted to call the sheriff, tell him everything that had happened since Coco's abduction, and take his lumps. He knew he was in over his head and was outgunned by Marcel and his gang of Tonton mutts. If he came clean, he could probably walk away from the events of last night. He laughed at his own naiveté. The blood and body count was too high to think he would be allowed to walk. Never happen. He, also, had to protect Max, Chief, and Coco from any trouble or fallout. Henrí and Rooster were a special problem that he wasn't sure how to handle. If the two Haitians went back to Miami, what would be their chance of survival? How long would it be until the Tonton found out that they were back in the 'hood' and unprotected?

The truth was Jack wanted to even the score with Marcel, one-on-one, for what happened to Coco. Laura—

Dr. Summers, gave Jack the top line report on Coco's condition a couple of hours ago, and it was worse than he had thought. In addition to internal injuries from the rape, she had a broken jaw, a concussion, and several broken ribs. Laura wanted to move her, immediately, to the Keys hospital, where she could receive the care she needed. Jack had vetoed that, and instead, demanded that she set up twenty-four-hour nursing care here at Laura's house.

"Look, you have to know a few R.N.'s you can trust that you can call in favors on. I'll pay whatever they ask. Don't worry about money."

"Jack, I'm not set up to treat injured patients here. She needs blood work, her jaw reset, ribs x-rayed, and, God knows, what else." Laura replied frustrated. She wanted to help but felt that she couldn't do as good a job here as she could at the hospital.

"Laura, if we take Coco to the hospital, the police will be there in minutes. I didn't tell you the whole story about what went down in Miami. I don't want to pull you into this. Just realize that we are in big trouble once word gets out. Trust me, it's better if we do this my way."

Laura had agreed to bring nursing help in along with a couple of doctor friends to analyze and treat Coco. Now that Chief had given Jack a heads up on the Sheriff's deputy, he was positive he had done the right thing.

Jack stood and stretched his sore aching muscles, and swallowed the last gulp of cold coffee. At the sink, he rinsed his cup then splashed his face with cold water, ripped off a few squares of paper towel, and slowly, dried off.

"Jack, there's a shower upstairs in the front guestroom, if you like," Laura said, as she came up and stood alongside of him.

"What I need is ten hours of sleep, then a shower and a change of clothes. But I have some errands to run."

"Where are you going? Is it safe to leave the house?"

"I need to move Max's cab away from the front of your house, ditch it somewhere, and then, I need to talk to a few people."

"How long will you be gone?" Laura asked, with concern in her voice.

"Just long enough to set a trap for a little black rat," Jack said.

Laura turned her back to the sink, so she was facing Jack and placed a hand on his chest. Her eyes softened. "Jack, be careful, you have a lot of people counting on you to make all this go away, me included. I'm scared, Jack. I'm not used to being in the middle of trouble like this. My life is orderly and quiet. I go to work every day, the gym three times a week, and to the supermarket. My idea of excitement is watching Dancing with the Stars on Tuesday nights. Then you come along and…and, then I don't know up from down."

Jack smiled, and covered her hand with his and squeezed. "Hang out with me long enough and you'll be a cigar-smoking, gun-toting member of Black Jack's gang, in no time. Play your cards right, and you may even become Black Jack's woman," he said.

"I don't smoke and I'm scared to death of guns, so, I guess I'll have to settle for being Black Jack's woman…for now," she said, as she bent closer to Jack's face, her eyes locking on his.

Jack's pulse kicked into max overdrive, Laura bent into him, with her head tilted. His fatigue evaporated and the pulsing headache disappeared, as he closed his eyes and met Laura half way. Her smell was intoxicating, her breath sweet and clean, and her taste delicious. He moaned, and pulled her in tight to his chest. Laura made small sounds, as she ran her hands over Jack's chest and shoulders, hungry for his smell and taste…

"Hey! Hey! You two break it up. Stop with the kissy face, I'm dying over here," Max said, standing on one foot in the kitchen doorway. "I think I need to see a real doctor. I'm scared I'm going to lose the leg, if I don't get to a hospital. No offense to you, Doc, but a couple of kisses on the booboo ain't going to cut it…"

Jack and Laura stepped back, embarrassed that they had been caught in a moment of intimacy. When Max's comments registered, they both confronted him.

"Hey, Max, knock that talk off. Dr. Summers fixed your wound up, first rate. You're not going to lose your leg. That's bull and you know it," Jack said, as he went to Max and led him to a chair. "Sit and take it easy and stay off the leg. You don't want it to start bleeding again."

"Mr. Simms, I can assure you that you will not lose your leg. It was a thru-shot that I swabbed and cleaned front to back, packed with antibiotics, and stitched up. You will be good as new, in a few days," Laura said.

"Yeah, then, why do I have this funny feeling that my leg ain't there? When I woke up, I couldn't feel nothin'. Gave me the frigging squirts."

"Max, that's the painkiller the Doc gave you to keep you out of pain. Jeez, haven't you ever been shot before? Quit your blubbering," Jack said, trying to relieve the tension and to get Max calmed down. He knew Max well enough to spot a string of insults and cheap shots were about to be unloaded.

"Missy Doctor, Uncle Henrí said for you to come. Ms. Coco is awake," Rooster said, from the doorway.

Henrí was talking to Coco when they entered the bedroom. Her eyes were groggy slits in her swollen face, as she listened to what was being told to her. Henrí was holding her hand with his mangled paw and patting her shoulder softly with the other as he spoke gently to her.

Henrí looked up, finished what he was saying to Coco, and said, "I was telling Coco about last night's events and what all the good doctor has done for us."

Laura hurried over and began checking Coco's vital signs. Jack stood on the other side of the bed, next to Henrí, staring down at Coco's beaten and bruised face and wanted to cry for this woman that was part of his Keys family. His emotions were bouncing around like a swimmer caught in whitewater. Anger raged, then subsided. Helplessness overwhelmed him, making his hands shake in frustration. But, overriding all the other emotions was desire for revenge. Revenge against the animals that had done this to someone he loved and was important to him. He vowed to himself that he would make Marcel Duvalier suffer for this.

"Jack, Jack, are you with us?" Laura said, concerned at the look on Jack's face.

"Yeah, I'm with you. Just tired I guess."

"I need to move Coco somewhere, so I can treat her internal injuries. We need to get her jaw set, x-rays of her chest to see if the broken ribs are doing any damage, then I need head x-rays of her skull to see how bad her concussion is...."

"Laura, we can't take the chance of going anywhere, you know that. On the one hand, we have Duvalier on our trail, and the other, we have a deputy that's looking for us. When they find us, there's going to be trouble, and I'm not talking legal trouble. I'm saying hurt locker trouble..."

"Jack, if we don't get this woman to a hospital, soon, we could have big problems that could put her in grave danger. I suspect that her concussion has bruised her brain, causing swelling, and, if it begins bleeding, we will need to relieve the pressure before it does irreversible damage. The longer we hold back from helping her, the lower her chances of survival."

Jack knew that Laura was right about medical care for Coco. It was, really, just a question of time before they would need to break out of hiding and either go on the offense or tuck tail and hunker down. His priority had to be Coco first. Everything else was secondary.

"Laura, we're still in danger, but I agree with you. What if we move Coco up to Marathon for treatment? Fisherman's Hospital is just as good as ours is here in

Key West. We can rent a van and make her comfortable for the fifty-mile trip. What do you think?"

"We should move her as little as possible, but, if you're really worried about being discovered by the sheriff, then I'll go along with you. Let's do it now, though. The sooner I can see what's going on inside her skull, the better," Laura said. "I've given her an anti-inflammatory shot that should stop any internal swelling…"

"Jackie, quick! Over here," Max stage-whispered.

Max held the blind open an inch, as he and Jack peered down at a sheriff's unit double-parked next to Max's taxi. The deputy was looking in the back windows and trying the doors, working his way around the car. Satisfied that no one was inside the van, the deputy stood staring at the house with one hand on his holstered pistol and the other working his shoulder radio.

"Jack, what is it?" Laura asked.

"We've got company. There's a sheriff's unit out front and it looks like he's calling for backup," Jack said, as he swung around, thinking fast. "Laura, go down and stall the guy…"

"Stall him? How? What should I say to him?"

"I don't know. Say anything. Just give us enough time to get out the back and into the alley."

Laura hurried downstairs and flung the front door open. "It's about time you guys showed up. I called two hours ago, about that piece of junk sitting in front of my house." Laura strode up to the deputy, fuming.

"I want that piece of junk out of here now. If you people can't handle a simple task like this, maybe I should call Commissioner Watts," she said, with her hands on her hips and chin stuck out.

"Whoa, little lady, slow down..." the deputy started.

"How dare you refer to me as *little lady*?" she spat, as she moved in close to him. "Evidently, you must think you are working Duval Street. You don't address me as anything but Doctor Summers, you got that...*Chubby*."

"Yes, Ma'am, uh...Doctor. We have a BOLO on this vehicle and I just assumed that perhaps the fugitives were holed up inside."

"I don't know what a bolo is, and I really don't care to find out...and I can tell you, with certainty, I don't have any fugitives in my house. Now, are you going to get this junk pile moved or do I need to call my friend, the commissioner?"

A sheriff's unit, with emergency lights whirling, flew around the corner, coming to a screeching halt, inches away from the pink taxi. A huge black man jumped out of the unit, pistol drawn, and ready for action.

Laura's brave front collapsed and she stepped back. Just the physical size of the officer was intimidating, but the pistol pointed at her was just too much and she broke down crying.

"What do we have, Benson?" Deputy Coltier asked, as he holstered his pistol.

"Some kind of mix up. The doctor here says she reported this abandoned vehicle a couple of hours ago, and thought I was here to arrange for towing," the deputy said, with a snicker as he watched Laura's demeanor melt into fear. "Said she was going to call County Commissioner Watts if we didn't get this wreck moved immediately."

Deputy Coltier moved in close to Laura. "I've seen you before. You work at the hospital, right?"

"Yes, I'm associated with the hospital, but I, also, see patients here," she said, as she pointed over her shoulder. She was beginning to regain her composure, once the pistol was holstered.

"Do you know the driver of this taxi?"

"I think everyone in Key West knows Max Simms. He's such a colorful character and part of the Key West scene…"

"He's an accessory to murder," Coltier said, bluntly. "How about his buddy, Jack Marsh? Do you know him?" Coltier was inching forward into Laura's space, becoming more intimidating with each word.

Laura seemed to be puzzled, and said, "Marsh. Sounds familiar. We had a man come into emergency the other night with a mild concussion. If I recall correctly, his name was Marsh...maybe Marchon, I can't remember."

"I don't believe in coincidence, Doc. I don't think this vehicle was left in front of your house just by chance. Let's go inside and look around," Coltier said, pushing Laura aside.

"You can't go in there, that's my home," she said, as she ran ahead of the big man and stood on the porch steps.

This brought her eye-to-eye with Coltier, and she was determined to stand her ground. Her hands started to shake and her voice trembled,

"You can't just go into a person's house. You need a search warrant..."

"Not when I have reasonable suspicion that felons are hiding inside. I don't need anything but this," he said, pulling his pistol out and wagging it under her nose.

"Now, step aside or I'll arrest you for interference with an officer in the pursuit of a felon."

Laura didn't have any idea how long she had been outside, and wasn't sure if Jack had enough time to get everyone out the back. Without thinking, she started screaming at the top of her lungs, *"Rape! Rape! Someone help me! Rape!"*

Deputy Coltier recoiled, in shock, as Laura fell into him and hung on to his pistol belt still screaming. Old Mrs. Dunleavy, from two doors up the block hurried down the sidewalk with a long barrel shotgun yelling, *"In the name of Jesus! Kick him in the nuts, Laura,"* she screamed out, *"You let go of her, or, I'll shoot your ass into kingdom come...Praise God!*

Deputy Benson, not knowing what to do, got back into his patrol unit and hunkered down over the steering wheel. Coltier was fighting to get away from Laura's grip, when Mrs. Donleavy unloaded with her shotgun. The thick door glass shattered into a million little diamonds, as the weapon's pellets tore by Coltier's head. Geez, this was misspelled Coulter!!!

Without thinking, he raised his pistol and cranked off a warning shot, and yelled, "Sheriff's Deputy, lay down your arms...Now!"

"The hell you say! In the name of Jesus, you lay down your arms!" Mrs. Donleavy yelled back, as she fumbled in her cardigan sweater for another shell.

Across the street in the graveyard, several homeless unkempt heads popped up from behind raised tombs and crypts to see what all the turmoil was.

"What's a fellow got to do to get some peace and quiet around here?" one old timer said, to no one in particular, as he tilted a half pint to his lips. He flopped down with his back to the marker, curious how this was going to play out.

Laura looked up and smiled, "I think you've met your match, Deputy. Mrs. Donleavy, ordinarily, doesn't miss, unless…she wants to."

The loud wailing of Deputy Benson's siren broke the silence freezing everyone in place.

"Everyone, lower your weapons and stand down," Benson said, over his unit's system. "I say again, cease fire, and lay down your weapons."

Mrs. Donleavy hesitated for a moment, and yelled back, "God's blood, man, he shot at me…he tried to kill me, death's angel just whizzed by my ear, not more than an inch away. Are you one of the devil's imps, too? By God! Rejoice!…*This is the day that the Lord hath made,*" she sang, loudly, as she swung the shotgun towards Deputy Benson.

"Halt! Don't shoot, I'm on your side," Benson called out from behind the front fender. *"Praise God! God is great! Hallelujah*! *Allahu Akbar*!" Benson yelled out, holding up his hands.

Coltier looked down at Laura, she released his waist, and he quietly, said, "You'll pay for this, lady, I promise. I'll have your ass bent over one of those tombstones over there, before I'm through with you."

Laura was scared but hid her fear behind a smirk. "You're wrong. I *own your ass*. It's my word against yours that you tried to rape me. I have a witness that saw you dragging me across the porch. You ever try to enter my house again or to threaten me, I'll be on the phone to every person I know in this county. Then, we'll see whose *ass* is bent over a tombstone. Now, please get off my porch and leave, before I call the commissioner."

Coltier snickered, and spat. "I know Marsh is here, or was here, and when I find out, either way, I'll be bumping your name to the top of my list. As for raping you, you would be begging me for more...*Laura*." He spat her name, as if it were something vile.

Laura watched him swagger out to Benson's unit and said something to him. Both men got in their patrol cars and sped away. Laura fell back into one of the rockers and started to cry.

"Are you ok, Laura, dear? Don't cry, it's over, they won't be back. If they do come back, we'll be ready for them. Praise Jesus."

Mrs. Donleavy sat next to Laura, rocking and letting the excitement and fear ebb away. Across the street, the cemetery was quiet and peaceful. The only movement was an old woman walking among the tombs with a bunch of flowers in her hand.

Chapter 21

Jack stood, craning his neck over Doc Robinson's shoulder, watching him run stainless wire through Coco's top gum. The old doctor paused to steady his hand, then fed the wire through the lower gum and pulled tight, drawing the top and bottom molars tightly together. He snipped the wire to equal lengths and deftly twisted them, tucking the two ends into the space between the teeth. Doc Robinson sat back, took a sip from his glass of gin, and wiped his mouth on his shirtsleeve.

"One more, on this side and we're through," he said to himself, belching a gin haze.

Jack straightened upright and stretched, before going out to the living room to give the others an update.

After the fast exit, out the back of Laura's house, the group had hustled down back alleys, with the intent of getting as much space between them and the sheriff's men as they could, before they sounded the alarm. Rooster carried Coco, effortlessly, as Jack helped Max hobble along. Henrí acted as point, giving the all clear sign a half block ahead of the others as they ran. Jack's plan was to try to make it, unseen, to the Sand Bar where they could hide, until he could put a plan together. He still thought that trying to make it to Fisherman's Hospital in Marathon was his best plan, but the problem was, how to get there? Deputy Coltier would only have to have a couple of patrol units sit on Highway 1 leading out of Key West to spot them and to pull them over. The other alternative was to have Chief Drummond pull the *Queen* alongside the dock, pick them up, and head for Boot Key Harbor in Marathon. By boat, they could be there before dark, which might work in their favor.

They had stopped to catch their breath at Duval and Truman, when suddenly a memory had popped into Jack's mind…of an old doctor who had worked the New Orleans boxing clubs and had moved to the Keys ten years ago. It was rumored, the doctor lost his license to practice medicine when a young up and coming middleweight fighter died after a ten-round fight from internal bleeding the doctor had failed to spot. The fighter was a white man with white money behind him, the doctor black, and in New Orleans, it did not take much imagination to figure out what was going to happen. The media tore him a new ass and when the dust settled, he had been stripped of his medical license, and ordered to leave town. Now, he lived in a small wood frame house in Little Bahama Town. He was known to see locals, occasionally, who wanted to stay below the radar or didn't have the money to see a "regular" doctor. Rumored, but never proven, was talk of treatment for gunshot wounds, stabbings, unlicensed drug treatment, family planning matters, and various other incidents found in poor and impoverished parts of towns and cities.

After catching their breath, Jack led his little troop to the doctor's house where, after a few minutes of introductions and explanations, Dr. Robinson took Coco into his small exam room and began treating her immediately. Now, Jack sat on the end of an old couch that had seen better days. The springs squeaked loudly as he sank down several inches, put his head back in exhaustion, and ran his hands over his tired eyes. Max was taking up half the couch, lying on his back and snoring loudly. Henrí was stretched out in an easy chair, also, asleep. He had a Bible open and resting on his chest, with a small smile on his age-creased face. Rooster was sitting in a rocker on the porch eating out of a box of Cheerios, seemingly, content, with his own company. Everyone was tired and at the end of his reserves. Jack knew, he had to find a safe place for a few days, to lay low and get everyone back on their feet.

"Mr. Marsh," Dr. Robinson said. "I think, we have Ms. Duvalier finished up. She is going to be fine. She just needs to stay off her feet, and sleep. I gave her a healthy shot that will keep her out for the next eight to ten hours." The old man laughed, and swallowed down the last inch of gin in his glass.

"Are you sure she will be okay? I thought, with a head injury, that you shouldn't give a person anything to knock them out..."

"Bah! Do not believe all that John Hopkins bull. That's just more of the medical system's moneymaking advice to keep you under their care longer. I worked with fighters all my life and never lost one to a concussion or brain injury. Sure, lots of cracked skulls and brains scrambled, but no deaths. Can I fix you a drink?" Dr. Robinson stood and headed for the kitchen, continuing to talk.

"The only man I came close to losing was a fighter named Mad Mike. He came out of the ninth ward, built like a bull, heavyweight class, stamina of a racehorse, but the thinnest skull I have ever seen on a man. It was at the City Auditorium over in Houston, a Friday night, and the place was packed. The noise was so loud, the ref had to walk to each corner, and yell, *Bell, Bell.*" He laughed, at the memory as he filled his water glass from a bottle of Bombay Gin. "The fighters came out, touched gloves, and it was over. Less than two seconds into the fight, the homeboy popped my man with a right to the forehead and *Crack*! My man went down like a two-hundred-pound bag of flour. The place went crazy, the crowd started booing, and throwing full cups of beer, glass bottles, chairs, and, anything else they could find. We grabbed our man and ran for the dressing rooms, as fast as we could, being pelted, and yelled at all the way. On the drive, back to New Orleans later that night, I thought we were going to lose him, but he pulled through. He's a little nutty now, but he's alive, preaches over in Orleans Parish."

"So, are you saying that Coco might have some mental issues after this?"

"Mr. Marsh, your friend doesn't have a concussion. Sure, she was pounded pretty hard, and, I know, she may not like me saying this, but she has one of the thickest skulls I've run across. She would have made a good lightweight, I'm thinking."

Jack felt a heavy weight lift off his shoulders. "No concussion. That is great news. What else did the x-ray show? Any swelling?"

"Oh, I'm sure she has swelling, but it's not serious. It'll go down in a day or two. As for her skull, I didn't need an x-ray. My visual evaluation and probing technique didn't reveal any fracturing or hairline cracks.

There is definitely bruising and subsurface swelling, but again, all that will go down in a few days."

"What do you mean by visual and probing technique, Doctor? Shouldn't you take an x-ray, to be sure?"

"Not necessary, Mr. Marsh. X-rays are another of the medical profession's ripoffs. Physical probing of the skull is as reliable as any sophisticated scanning out there. I was taught this by one of the smartest medical professors that ever-taught medicine at Tulane," he chuckled. "Professor Gates called it his Watermelon Procedure...Thump. Feel. Listen." Dr. Robinson grinned, tossing down his gin.

"You're kidding, right?" Jack was aghast at the doctor's flippant attitude. Coco's life was at stake.

"Not at all. It is a widely-used procedure, especially, in rural and under developed areas, where medical practice is still, an esteemed profession and not all these richie-rich specialists, driving medical costs out of sight. If things don't get back to basics in the medical field, I'm afraid the government will stick its nose into it and then things will really be mucked up. Now, follow me, and we'll check on your other friends."

Dr. Robinson sat on the couch and lifted Max's leg into his lap. "Umm-hmm, gunshot wound. Looks like maybe a small caliber, a woman's piece. We used to call them shooflies back in the day. Nasty little buggers, big enough to hurt like hell, but not big enough to kill."

"You saying I ain't going to die, Doc!" Max struggled to sit upright. "Well, I got news for you, you're the second quack I've seen in the last few hours, and you're both full of it. If I don't get a transfusion in me of some fresh blood, I'm going to croak. You don't know the pain I'm in. If I thought you were a legit doctor, I would sue in a heartbeat. I would own this...this clinic and everything in it."

Dr. Robinson threw his head back laughing. "Jack, is this man as dumb as he sounds? He wants this place! My goodness, I better check him for lead poisoning. Something's affected his brain."

Jack laughed, along with the doctor, "I'll admit, strange things roll off that man's tongue, most at the wrong time, but we love him. We're the only people that will put up with his wacky rants.

"Hey Jackie, what are you saying? I'm not good enough for you guys? You'd think I'm duck liver or something the way you talk..."

"Take it easy, Max; I was just busting your chops. Back off and relax."

"Mr. Marsh, first chance you get, feed this man a couple of well-marbled ribeye steaks, nice and rare. He'll feel like running a marathon, once he gets that red meat in him," Dr. Robinson said. "Now, tell me what's wrong with the big fellow on the porch."

"Rooster? I don't really know much about him. I just met him and his mother yesterday…"

"That's not his mother," Henrí said, setting the Bible on the side table. "Momma Dey took him in, when he was four or five years old. Found him on one of the garbage dumps around Port-au-Prince. The child was standing, in a trance, no clothes, no nothing. She raised him like her own. We tried to find out something about him by the tattoo on his hand and the scar on the top of his head, but never got to the bottom of it."

Dr. Robinson went to the screen door and called for Rooster to come in. Inside, Dr. Robinson sat Rooster in a straight back chair, bent forward, began a visual exam, checking his eyes and ears, listened to his heart, and then went back to the eyes.

"Rooster, follow my finger, as I move it," he said, moving his finger to the right and left, then up and down. "What number comes after five, Rooster?"

"Momma says six comes after five." Rooster responded, immediately.

"What does Rooster say comes after five?"

Rooster stared ahead, in thought, "Rooster doesn't know," was his answer.

"What's Rooster's favorite color?"

Again, Rooster concentrated hard on the question. "Rooster doesn't know colors."

"What is Momma's favorite color?"

"Red, oh yes. Red is her favorite color," he said, smiling.

Dr. Robinson stood and took Rooster's hands in his, massaging them gently, then turned them over, palm up. He stared at the Voodoo symbol of the Eye of Death tattooed on the right palm. On closer exam, he saw that the tips of the fingers, on both hands, were smooth from the first joint to the nail. Rooster did not have any fingerprints. He reached over and pushed Rooster's head down until his chin rested on his chest. His fingers worked busily at the hair on the crown, stopping only when he found what he was looking for.

"Take a look, Mr. Marsh," Robinson said, as he ran his fingers over the scar tissue in the shape of a pantograph. "I think I have found what our big friend's problem is. I have read and heard about this, but until now, I thought it was just more Voodoo mumbo-jumbo." Did you mean pantograph? Look it up on google, did you mean pentagram, devil icon?

"What is it, Doc?" Max was on his feet, bending in to see what all the fuss was about.

"More island witchcraft. It just doesn't go away. Would you believe that two out of three of my local patients practice Voodoo? They take all these old African secret remedies for every ailment under the sun, but then when things get worse, they show up here looking for help." He sat on the sofa and cleaned his glasses on the corner of the throw cover. "By necessity, I have had to study some of the more common salves, unguents, and balms the local priests use, just so I'll know how to treat the patients when they come in with whatever complaint they have. In the process, I have read about some of the dark side of the practice, the black arts that have been around for hundreds of years going back in time, farther than the ancient pyramids of Egypt."

"So, what does that have to do with Rooster?" Jack asked.

"I'm not totally sure of my facts, yet, but I think, Rooster must have been given something, as a child that put him into this semi-catatonic state. For what purpose, I cannot say. Although there are studies, done by experts in the field, that show cyanide was often used to place people in a wakeful sleep, the poison acts as a long-term hypnotic. The individual can function, physically, but, not mentally. He is susceptible to outside commands and influences, but is almost in a vegetative state when left to his own devices."

"Are you saying Rooster is a zombie, Doc?" Max asked, wide-eyed.

"Yes and no, Max. I know that something is happening inside his brain. There are signs of intelligence, but I don't think he is the one controlling it. Perhaps, over the years, this Momma Dey has taught him to do repetitive tasks and basic communication skills, but there is still a major disconnect going on," Doc said.

"Is he dangerous, ya think?" Max asked.

"He doesn't appear to be. I guess it depends on what Momma Dey programmed him to do. There are probably triggers that need to be tripped which signal specific responses. The only person who knows those triggers is Momma Dey…and, of course, Rooster."

"Well, this is all very interesting, but we'll just have to roll with it for now, Doc," Jack said. "Maybe after things settle down, we can get together again, and discuss what we can do for Rooster. But as soon as possible, we need to move this circus down the road."

"No problem. I completely understand. Meanwhile, I have a friend at Tulane who heads up the Department of Psychiatry. I will talk with him, and see if we can't come up with something to help this fellow."

"That's great Doc. I'm going to call one of my people over with a van to pick us up, and we'll get out of your hair. What do you figure I owe you for all you've done for us?"

"Oh, Mr. Marsh, don't even bother yourself. It's been a long time since I was part of a mystery. What you people did, and where you are going from here, is best kept a secret. What I don't know, I can't tell or talk about...if asked. But, if you did feel so inclined to leave a little token of appreciation of my medical skills behind, I would prefer it was cash. Paper trails tend to trip up the best of alibis, wouldn't you agree?"

Jack smiled, and stepped out on the porch to call Lamont.

"This is the Sand Bar, Manager speaking," Lamont's familiar voice said, politely.

"Manager! What did you do while I was gone, give yourself a promotion?"

"Jack! Mr. Marsh! You're alive. Damn, Man, why didn't you call? We've been worried sick, Junior, and me. I swear if you weren't the boss, I would kick your ass for making me worry like that. Where you been...where are you...when are you coming home?" Lamont was almost screaming into the phone.

"OK, OK, calm down and listen up. I need you to pick up a rental van from the airport, as soon as we hang up. Once you have the van, swing over to Little Bahamas and Doc Robinson's clinic. We'll be waiting for you. Got all that?"

"Sure, no problem. Bounce over to the airport and check out a van. But, what are you doing at that old quack's place? Don't tell me you caught one of those social diseases and you needed some discreet help," Lamont laughed.

"Not funny, Lamont. Keep your mind on the task. I'm not in the mood for your wit, right now. Tell Cookie to load up a couple of coolers with enough food out of the reefer to last a few days. Tell him to throw in some steaks and hamburger meat. And Lamont, don't let anyone follow you here," he said before he hung up.

His next call was to Chief Drummond.

"Yeah."

"Chief, it's me. Listen up. We'll be at the dive shop in about thirty minutes. If you haven't already, bring the *Queen* up alongside, and be ready to take us aboard and haul ass. We're going out on the blue for a few days, until things cool down."

"No problem, she's shipshape and ready. I figured you might want to get lost for a while, so, I topped off the fuel and fresh water tanks. I even have a bunch of albacore steaks thawing. The sooner we shake Key West's dust off, the better.

"Good man, Chief. If you get there before us, go down in the shop's cellar and bring up a couple of rifles and a few pistols and ammo, just in case we run into our Tonton buddies out there."

"No problem, Kemo-sabe. But, I don't think we'll run across anyone we know, that is, unless you have something else banging around inside that devious mind of yours. Anything you want to share with me?"

"Not just yet. I'm just bouncing options around. It looks like Coco is going to pull through, and, the rest of us are just dinged up with nothing permanent keeping us from a little payback. I need some sleep and then we'll talk things over."

"Sounds good. I think we could all use about ten hours of uninterrupted sleep. Maybe, we should drop anchor out in the Tortugas. No one would mess with us there. The water is nice and calm, the storm has blown itself out, and the latest NOAA report is that we'll have clear and sunny skies for the next week."

"Go ahead, and plot your course, but, also, lay one out for Rat Key, just as a fall back."

"Ah ha, now, I can see which way the wind's blowing. Lying off Rat Key in the Bahamas channel gives us a straight shot up to Bimini. Oh, Jack, you're a clever one all right."

"Keep it to yourself, Bull. I want everyone to relax for a couple of days, before we move back into action. A little time might lull Marcel into dropping his guard, too."

Chapter 22 Spacing has gone haywire on sides

Deputy Coltier sat on the hood of his pickup, watching, as the Range Rover pulled into the turnout at mile marker 16. The Rover kicked up a cloud of coral dust, when it came to a quick stop, two feet away from Coltier. He could see the stupid laugh on the driver's face and his four companions, with their glazed-over eyes and exaggerated grins. Coltier swore under his breath. Coltier hated being dirty. Having the smallest speck of dust on him, or his gear, made him cringe. When he made landfall on Fort Lauderdale's public beach ten years ago, after spending thirty-two days adrift with nineteen other political refugees from Haiti, he swore, he would never be poor, hungry, or dirty again. Within two weeks of landing and escaping into the Miami quagmire of racial stew, he had killed a man and assumed his identity, his background, and his possessions. His victim had an affinity for young black males that Coltier spotted, immediately, for what he was and moved in on him. He strangled the man, drove him out to the Everglade swamps, and dumped him after slicing him open to attract the gators. Going into that evening, he had been Edward Plantier. By eleven that night, he emerged as Bolivar Coltier, a U.S. citizen with a naturalized Cuban refugee father and Haitian mother. He was safe. Fix this below spacing.

"Yes, yes, we are here, the Conch man can relax," the tall, lanky gangsta said, as he stepped out of the passenger seat.

Coltier wanted to smash the man's face for the disrespect in his manners, his haughty demeanor, the fact that he was high on something and wobbled, as he approached. The others, who fell in behind, were copies of their leader, all skinny, with baggy island shirts, stovepipe jeans, and sandals. A cloud of blue smoke floated above them, as they slouched forward. Coltier had a quick mental picture of a pack of hyenas on the African Savannah, casually, approaching their unsuspecting prey. He knew these men to be stone hard killers who would turn on each other for the fun of it or for a few dollars from their master, Marcel Duvalier.

"So, Paul LeClerc, we meet again," Coltier said, with a forced smile on his face. "It has been a while since we have worked together. I hope all is well between you and your...husband." Coltier could not resist hurling the insult.

"Careful, Bolivar, my men are hungry for some fun. I think it best that you never mention that subject again. Besides, that is ancient history. We were young, we did dumb things, and we each did what we had to do to stay alive in those days."

"Whatever you say, LeClerc. Is this the best crew you could pull together? I told Marcel to send me a good team, not a bunch of potheads," Coltier said, studying the four men.

It was hard to believe that he was anything like these punks at one time. He shuddered at the memory of his teen years as a hit man for the Tonton and the carnage he and his friends caused. Even Jean Claude 'Baby Doc' Duvalier, when he was still President, was appalled by his ruthlessness. Those had been terrible years for Coltier, growing up in the slum rubble that was next to an open garbage pit. The only way out of such poverty was by killing or being killed. His escape from the Island to Miami should have been the beginning of a new life. Instead, within a year, he was back under the Tonton's murderous thumb. This time, Marcel 'Little Doc' Duvalier found him and threatened to expose him to the authorities for murdering the real Bolivar Coltier in Miami, stealing his identity. Coltier had to agree to do Marcel's bidding, if, and when, he ever required it, in return for silence. Over the past decade, he had been called twice by Marcel to maintain that silence. Both times were assassinations on rich Haitian businessmen and their wives, living in Miami. Both times, Coltier had been paid twenty thousand dollars and ordered to disappear back into his hidey-hole in Key West.

"My brother, for you, Marcel sends only the best of the best. We are known as the Magnificent Five," the glassy eyed killer said, not bothering to wipe white spittle from the corners of his mouth. "My instructions are to do whatever you command us to do. Do it quickly, quietly, and then to disappear back to Babylon, Hahaha."

Coltier knew that the reference to Babylon was what most Islanders called the white man's world. He never used the term himself, but sympathized with those who did. There was no love lost, regardless of what the travel agencies spit out about the smiling Island people. Coltier felt there was nothing the white man ever did for the Caribbean people, other than, to keep them under their heel and treat them as inferiors when visiting the home islands.

Coltier slid off the truck's hood and motioned with his forefinger to come near, "Step in close, all of you, because, I'm going to say this only once." Coltier cleared his throat of coral dust and spat. "Key West is not Port-au-Prince. You can't shoot the place up and you can't take anything that doesn't belong to you. While you are here, you will do *exactly* as I say. If I don't say to do something, then you don't do it. Understood?'

"Who's this doing all this yakking 'bout do dis, do dat? You're not talking to a mess of Bahama boys. You're talking to the Magnificent Five…"

Striking out as quick as a viper, Coltier picked the man up by his throat and squeezed. "You weren't listening, *meat*. I said, I am in charge and I don't think I asked for comments, or back talk."

The man hung, helplessly, clawing, at Coltier's chokehold, fighting for air. The other men backed up a couple of steps in alarm at the quickly developing situation, then just as quickly, stepped forward to come to the aid of their friend. Coltier pulled a long barreled .357 out of his waistband and pointed it at LeClerc's head.

"You want to be the first to go, Paul? You, punks, listen to me. You fuck with me and I'll cut you down. Did LeClerc tell you who I am? Did he tell you that I've killed men for just looking at me? Did he tell you that I almost killed him for stealing a cold pizza crust from me when we were kids?" The arteries on Coltier's neck were thick and bunched as his temper built.

LeClerc had seen Coltier lose his temper in the past, and he knew there was going to be a killing. He needed to say something to bring him back from the edge.

"I told them, Edward. I told 'em that you are one crazy mutha and to watch their selves around you," he said. "These are all good men. They're just what you wanted to get this job done. Just give them a few minutes to let the ganja burn off and they'll be fine."

Coltier shook the man one more time and let him drop to the ground. His head swiveled over to LeClerc, with the madness still in his eyes, "Don't ever call me Edward again! My name is Bolivar Coltier."

The thugs stood silent and very docile, in a half circle around the front of the pickup, kicking at the coral, watching as cars whizzed by on the highway. Coltier took several deep breaths to calm his rage. "You're here to help me get my hands on one man, Jack Marsh. You will not kill him; you will not hurt him. He belongs to Marcel. My job is to deliver him to Marcel, unharmed and alive. The second objective is a Haitian woman who has information that Marcel and his Father need," Coltier said, through gritted teeth. "Little Doc told me, personally, if we failed to bring the man and the woman to him as commanded, he would see us all skinned, and we all know that Marcel doesn't make idle threats."

Chapter 23

"Something's wrong, Lamont. Slow down," Jack cautioned, as they pulled onto Laura's street.

"What is it, Jack?" Max asked, sitting forward and peering over Jack's shoulder.

"I'm not sure, Max," Jack said, as he strained forward trying to understand what had set off alarms in his brain. "Back up and pull around the cemetery."

A minute later, Lamont eased the van under the shade of an ancient tamarind tree and cut the engine. Everyone sat, quietly, except for Coco, who was snoring softly through her broken nose. Rooster held Coco's head in his lap and lovingly stroked her hair with his huge hand as he cooed.

Jack got out, crossed the sidewalk, and stood behind a raised crypt. The front of Laura's house appeared the same, but something was out of place that Jack couldn't put his finger on. After a moment, he spotted a man in the deep shadows sitting in one of the porch rockers. The man was partially hidden by the lush jasmine vines that had taken over the trellis on that side of the porch. Jack watched, for a few minutes, while he thought about this turn of events. Laura had to be inside. The question was who was in there with her, and what were they doing to her? He scanned the street and saw a Range Rover parked towards the corner that didn't fit in. The giveaway was all the colored party beads hanging from the mirror and a large Rasta silhouette-sticker on the window of the rear door. He went back to the van and stuck his head in.

"Lamont, take everyone over to the *Queen*. Make sure no one sees you or follows you. Got it? When you get there, tell Chief to wait an hour for me back out on the anchorage. I'll take a water taxi, if I'm coming. After an hour, he should go to the first site we talked about earlier and I'll meet him there when I can."

"Sure, Jack, but what about you? Are you walking into trouble? I can go with you and let Max drive the van over to meet Chief."

Jack knew that the men inside were dangerous and, unless he could get inside, unseen and grab Laura, he was going to be in a tight fix.

"Max, is your leg good enough to drive the van?" Jack asked, deciding that Lamont's suggestion made good sense.

"Sure, but I want to stay with you and duke it out with those humps. If that little midget's inside there I want him...he is mine, Jack...he is mine." Max drug out the last three words, as he punctuated the air with his finger.

"Max, I need you to take care of everyone, get them over to the *Queen*, and report into Chief Drummond. Now, let's move it. Laura's in danger."

Jack and Lamont stood behind a crypt, scoping out the Rover across the street. They had made their way across the cemetery, with no problem other than a drunk who they scared the hell out of when he awoke and saw Jack standing over him with his gun pointed at his head. Jack put his finger to his mouth for silence and the old bum shook his head in understanding.

"There's five of 'em, Mister. I seen 'em go inside about thirty minutes ago, mean looking sumsabichez. Black as midnight, too. Got them watermelon hats on, everyone of 'em, with a mouth full of gold teeth, and guns like I ain't seen since the Nam. Deputy Coltier pulled up in his pickup, did a slow roll-by, pointed out the house, and then drove off."

"Did you see the woman that lives there?"

"You mean Doc Laura? Nah, she's at the widow's house, been there since the shootout with that mean ass cop, Coltier. I watched the old widow with that damn shotgun of hers in one hand and Doc Laura by the arm with the other. Both of 'em scared, and looking around like they expected the angel of death to swoop down at any time."

Jack pulled a few bills out of his pocket and gave them to the old man. "Thanks, old timer, you've been a big help. Now, scoot out of here. That angel might show up and you won't want any part of it."

"Well, thanks, Mister, that's nice of you to help out an old vet..." The old man was, quickly, getting choked up. "I won't forget this. I never forget a kindness...or a face...Semper Fi, Mac."

"No thanks necessary. Now scoot. We have work to do," Jack said, helping the old man up.

Jack watched the old vet disappear through the crypts and tombs, hunched over and alert for booby-traps and snipers. *"He has a few bucks in his pocket and he's making his bird out of the bush."* Jack smiled, at the jargon used by every field marine since Vietnam.

It took about ten minutes to work their way around to the side of the widow's house and creep through her orchard of key lime, mango, and banana trees. The yard was lush with every variety of tropical plant and flower imaginable. It was a secluded paradise of greens, purples, and reds, the air rich with a golden pollen haze and nose-running aromas that left the pallet with a sugary taste. Jack gasped, and sneezed, so hard, his neck popped. A second later, he sneezed again...then again.

"God's Blood! You keep sneezing like that and those fellows down the street will be up here to see what all the explosions are about. Now get in here, the both of you," the widow said, shooing them inside with her shotgun.

Jack and Lamont obeyed, not out of fear of the shotgun, but for the little woman that wore her hair in a tight bun and the rimless spectacles perched on her nose.

This was a woman that one just, naturally, does what she says to do.

"Wipe those feet. I won't abide slovenliness in my house and don't want it all tracked up by a couple of knuckleheads."

"Yes, ma'am," Lamont said, as he unconsciously put Jack between himself and the widow.

"Praise God, but you're a big one. Laura said you were tall and handsome, but I wasn't expecting Goliath," she said, as she squeezed Jack's biceps in admiration. "I'll bet you was a soldier boy once, to have all those muscles, weren't you, Jack?" she said sweetly.

"Yes, Ma'am, I was in the Marines, for a while, but, that was a long time ago." Jack felt his face flush red under the widow's scrutiny. If he did not know better, he would think she was checking him out. *"Nah, that's sick, Jack, you're always thinking the chicks are hot for you. This is an old lady."*

"...I've always been big; I guess God just made me this way," Jack stuttered.

"The Lord gives to each..." she said, shifting her attention to Lamont. "Come out from behind Jack and let me take a look at you. What's your name?"

"Lamont," he whispered, as he stepped around Jack and hung his chin on his chest.

The widow reached out and pulled him closer to her, looking him over, feeling his shoulders, muscled arms, and chest.

"Do you know Jesus, Lamont? Do you read His Holy Word? Have you been baptized in the Spirit?" she asked, as she pulled his head into her bosom and held it tight. "The world is a wicked place and without the Lord, we are all nothing but sinners. Are you a sinner, Lamont? Tell me child, talk to me, tell me your sins."

"Uh...I ain't got none, Miss Widow, I swear it. I...uh, quit sinning, once I found out what happens to sinners."

"*Praise God!*" the widow yelled loudly. "Lord, we have us a sinner *and* a liar in our mist...he was lost, but now he is found, *Praise Jesus!*"

"Uh, excuse me, ma'am, but I need to see Laura and get going. We have a rather pressing deadline we are up against," Jack said.

Without relinquishing her hold on Lamont, the widow craned her neck and said breathlessly, "Upstairs, the bedroom on the right."

Before Jack was out of the room, the widow had shifted her hold and was hotly whispering salvation in Lamont's ear.

Jack's heart skipped a beat, as he stood in the bedroom doorway, looking at Laura lying on the bed, beautiful with her eyes closed, her face relaxed in peace. He closed the door, walked softly across the room, and sat on the edge of the bed.

"Laura," he whispered, so softly he wasn't sure that he had said anything. Suddenly his eyes were wet with tears and a hollow longing filled his chest. He had never felt emptiness like this before, an ache so strong he moaned in grief. Of all the women he had known, why was this one so different? Why did he feel this way about her, what was special that set her off from the others? Maybe, he was just tired and this feeling was part of coming down off the rush of the last few days.

Laura opened her eyes and smiled. She reached up, pulled Jack to her, whispered his name, and he knew then, this was real. There was no going back. This is what he had been looking for most of his life and now that he found it, he wasn't letting go. No one was going to screw this up for him, especially him.

"Laura, we have to get out of here," he whispered. She was soft and clean, the smell of honeysuckle strong in his nose. "I came back to get you, before Coltier and his goons get their hands on you. They are inside your house looking for us. We need to disappear for a few days, until I can get things under control."

"I'm scared. Jack, don't let them get me. That Deputy scared me so bad this morning, it made me throw up. Don't ask me to do something like that again, promise me, Jack."

"I won't, I promise. I won't let anyone hurt you, ever," Jack said. "I'm sorry. Believe me, I never should have gone to your place last night. For some reason, I just knew in my heart that I needed to see you, to be with you."

"I know, I feel the same way, Jack..."

"Let's roll, Boss. We have company in the alley," Lamont said, as he burst into the room.

Jack's pulse redlined, he ran to the window and peeped out through the blinds. Coltier's pickup was slowly cruising the alley, two gun mutts stood in the bed of the truck, craning their necks, checking each backyard. He dropped the shade, ran to the front hall window, and looked out. The Rover was parked in front of the widow's, both front doors open with the radio blaring Jamaican Rap

"Lamont, take Laura, and on my signal, run out the front door, grab Max's taxi, then haul ass to the *Queen*," Jack shouted out, running down the stairs.

"What about a key?"

"Max keeps a spare in the ashtray. Now, get ready."

Laura was scared, her hands were shaking, as she ran them through her hair. "What about you? What are you going to do?" she asked, with concern.

"I'm going to throw a monkey wrench into their plans. Now, come on."

Lamont and Laura followed Jack to the front door and watched him ease out on the front porch, looked both ways, and signaled them to run.

"What about Mrs. Bennett?" Laura asked, turning to go back.

"She's fine. She's in her sewing room taking a snooze. There's a little daybed in there, she said she was really tired and wanted to catch twenty winks. Let her rest," Lamont said, and threw a guilty look at Jack, shrugging his shoulders.

With that, the two rushed down the street to Max's taxi and jumped in. A second later, a cloud of blue oily smoke belched out of the tailpipe and lunged forward, chugged a couple of times, then smoothed out and picked up speed.

Jack watched until the taxi was around the far corner, then ran to the Rover. The keys were in the ignition and the motor was idling. An Uzi was on the floorboard, on the passenger side, and Jack scooped it up, checking the action. The Israeli automatic was old and scratched up with most of the bluing long-gone. He dropped the magazine out, saw that it was full, and popped it back in the receiver. A movement in the rearview mirror caught his eye, and in the same instant, he threw the Rover into reverse and floored it. The powerful engine lunged, throwing Jack into the steering wheel. Quickly, he recovered, jammed the gas down, making the tires scream and burn rubber as he steered, directly, for the two men he had spotted running toward him. The two mutts skidded to a stop and dove out of the way. One of them was not fast enough and was thrown under the back wheel making the Rover bounce as it rolled over him. There was a sharp scream, then the front wheels hit the body and the Rover was clear.

Jack whipped the steering wheel, sharply, to the left, throwing the Rover into a severe ninety-degree curve. He got the vehicle under control, crammed the shift into low gear, and shot forward, aiming for the second man.

The man was standing over his companion's torn body in disbelief. This was not supposed to be the way things happened. They were Tonton, nobody fucked with Tonton, much less run over them like a speed bump in the road. At the last second, he looked up and saw a ton and a half of plastic and aluminum bearing down on him with some crazy Babylonian behind the wheel. He raised his pistol and fired into the man's face. The windshield shattered but the vehicle kept coming. He pointed, squeezed the trigger, and his world went black.

Jack kept the vehicle under control, as the windshield shattered into a million little cubes of safety glass. He felt, more than he saw, the man that was shooting at him hit the hood and fly over the top. He looked back to see the body roll to a stop, unmoving. At the corner, he floored the SUV, drove two blocks, and turned into an alley. Jack checked the glove box for registration or insurance, but came up empty. His hand touched something soft and he pulled out a large Ziploc baggie filled with cocaine. He put his hand back inside and pulled out a fat envelope filled with cash. Nothing was planned, he was just following his instincts. He jammed the envelope of cash into his front pocket, then swiped his hand over the dashboard clearing off all the broken glass. He ripped open the kilo bag and poured it over the dash then spread it out evenly. Using his index finger, he wrote,

C-A-Y-M-A-N-B-R-A-C...a/c1357913   *Grandma Duvalier why the a/c?*

He sat back, inspecting his handiwork and thinking, *"A lot of people have been killed for this information and before anyone spends any of the money, if there is any, more will die.* Satisfied, he got out of the

SUV, rubbed his gums with his finger to get rid of the residue of coke. The hit was sharp and fast, the weariness rolled off him and he felt wide-awake and alert, the effects of the powder. He smiled, zipped the bag closed, and stuffed it and the Uzi into a paper bag from the back seat. He tucked it under his arm, then hurried down the alley on foot cutting through backyards.

Chapter 24

Deputy Coltier wanted to kill. It didn't matter whom, he just wanted to reach out and strangle someone. Jack Marsh was the target of his wrath, but, he was nowhere to be found. He was in the wind, hunkered down somewhere in this God-forsaken town, but, where? The only solace was the message Marsh had left on the Rover's dash.

When Coltier had heard the gunshots and screeching tires, he and LeClerc were parked in the alley behind the widow's house. He rushed around the corner, saw the two dead bodies, and immediately, knew what had happened. LeClerc jumped out, and with the help of his two teammates, threw the bodies in the bed of the truck, pounded on the roof, yelling for Coltier to move it. Just by chance, to get away from the area, Coltier took the same route as Marsh. He sped by the alley that Jack had just departed from, saw the Rover out the corner of his eye, and slammed on the brakes. The other three men in the truck bed saw the Rover and jumped from the truck as it screeched to a stop with their pistols out and ready for revenge.

Coltier yelled, "LeClerc, circle the block. You, stay with the truck," he pointed to the third man. "Follow me, but don't shoot. We want him alive."

Now, as he sat behind the steering wheel, looking at the message on the dash, he began to smile. This had to be the information that Marcel has been after from the beginning. This was not just about wanting Jack Marsh and Coco Duvalier taken alive so he could have his way with them. No, this had to be bigger than that. Coltier knew about Marcel's father, Jean-Claude 'Baby Doc' Duvalier, wanting to be head of the Haitian government again. Jean-Claude would need a lot of money to pay off his friends and officials to regain the presidency. Marcel's role was to find the money, to eliminate any competition running against his father, and to use the Tonton Macoute as a force to bring the populace into line. When his father became head of the government again, Marcel would be unfettered to do as he pleased throughout the country. Another reign of terror was about to be unleashed upon the people of Haiti.

Coltier's smile disappeared as the Duvaliers plan fell into place in his mind. The magnitude of the plan surprised him, knowing that Marcel was not mentally capable of putting something like this together on his own. Marcel's power grew from his audacity and ruthlessness, his maniacal pleasure of killing, and inflicting pain. This had to be his father's master plan and Marcel was just the tip of the sword.

This Duvalier plan was about money, big money, and what a better place to hide it than in plain sight? Grandma Duvalier, the old Voodoo Priestess herself, had thought ahead and siphoned money off from her crazy old husband, Papa Doc, while he was alive, in hopes that, someday, her son or grandsons would take back power in Haiti. It was farfetched maybe, but, what else made sense? Even Marsh's involvement fell into place. Marcel's men kidnapped Coco Duvalier from the Sand Bar, took her to Miami, and tried to get information about the location of her grandmother's war chest. Marsh went in pursuit and shot up the Haitian compound, getting Coco back from her captors, and headed south back to the Keys. That is when Marcel had called him, said he was sending a team down and he was to bring Marsh and the girl back to him, alive.

Coltier saw LeClerc coming up from the street and quickly wiped his hand across the dashboard, erasing Marsh's message. Without thinking his plan through, he knew what he had to do.

"LeClerc, come up here, we've got problems," Coltier said, as he slid out of the driver's seat. "We need to get your vehicle out of the area, like right now."

"Look at my beautiful baby! I've only had it a couple of weeks," LeClerc wailed, taking in the damage to the windshield and the dented hood where one of the dead had hit it and tumbled over the top, leaving a bloody trail.

Coltier called out to the other men, telling them to bring the bodies from the truck bed and throw them in the back of the Rover.

"Where am I supposed to drive to? I can't be driving this thing with no windshield. Number one, it could be dangerous, and two, what if I get stopped by a cop?"

Coltier smirked and said, "You never were very bright, Paul. Drive over to Sears Town, park it, and boost another one."

"Yeah, sure, that's cool," LeClerc smiled, stupidly as he turned the ignition key. "What should I do then? Where are we going to meet up?"

Coltier closed the rear passenger door as the skinny guy named Crow slid in. He didn't know the name of the one riding shotgun and didn't care to know it. The smackhead was off in another world, bouncing his upper body to some imaginary beat. Coltier smiled at Crow as he raised his throw-down piece, an untraceable .38 auto, and shot the man in the face. He shifted his arm and popped the bouncer in the side of the head with one round, then put the pistol at the base of LeClerc's skull,

"Sorry, Paul, party's over," he said, and pulled the trigger.

Thirty minutes later, both ends of the alley were taped off with bright yellow crime scene tape and uniformed cops flagging the curious on. Sheriff Taylor was smoking a cigarette staring at the crime scene, as Coltier repeated his story for the second time.

"And then you backed up, saw the deceased sitting here in the Rover, and approached to investigate. Is that correct?"

"Yes Sir. I thought it was suspicious, to begin with, for an expensive car like this to be just sitting in the alley. When I approached on foot I knew, immediately, something was wrong. No one was moving, nothing. I thought, maybe they saw me approaching and were afraid I was going to bust them on a vagrancy. Then, when I got closer, I saw all this blood and the cocaine powder all over the place. That's when I called it in."

"You did well, Coltier. The only comment I would make is that in the future when you come up on bangers like these that you call for backup before approaching.

Other than that, you did well. Keep it up," Sheriff Taylor said, and walked over to talk to the Navy CSI team on loan from the Boca Chica Navy Base.

"Are we in agreement here, Commander?" the sheriff asked.

"They don't come any simpler than this, Sheriff. This is your standard drug deal gone bad. A carload of bad asses drives down from Miami to do their deal, the other team shows up, the money doesn't match the merchandise, or vice versa, and Bang-Bang, the deal falls apart."

"Exactly my thinking too, Commander. I just wish those mutts would stay up north to carry out their business. Key West gets a bad rap, every time something like this goes down."

Chapter 25

Deputy Coltier wanted to run back to his pickup and flee the crime scene to avoid the sheriff asking any more questions. He had to control himself from breaking into a sprint to get away before the truth became obvious. He smiled, inwardly, at how easy it had been to fool the sheriff with that story about a drug deal gone bad, and how quickly the CSI people went along with the sheriff and chalked it up to just some monkey-ass thugs killing each other off. As far as they were concerned, this was a closed case and wouldn't spend another minute examining the scene to find out what really happened here in the alley.

Coltier lived in a singlewide trailer by himself on Shrimp Road, off Highway 1, outside of Key West. The trailer was a present to himself with the money from one of the hit jobs he had done for Marcel a couple of years earlier. Compared to the cardboard shack where he was raised in, this place was a castle. He took great pride in keeping it clean and tidy at all times, almost showroom quality, inside and out. The trailer park was cut out of mangrove swamp, the grounds filled in with oyster shell, and crushed coral. The owner of the park could have cared less about privacy and packed in trailers as tight as he could squeeze them. Coltier's plot was at the very end of the packed-in trailers, so he had some degree of privacy facing out on the remaining mangroves.

Coltier slowed to a roll, turned in under his carport awning, and cut the motor. He drove straight home from the crime scene, anxious to get inside and take care of business. He was beginning to feel the bugs crawling around inside his head that would soon be screaming for attention. He did a quick walk around the trailer looking for any telltale signs of intruders, then went inside. His eyes were tearing and burning now and the coke bugs were coming to life under the skin of his arms and chest.

Another few minutes and he would be on the floor screaming in agony. His head ticked spasmodically, as he moved into the small kitchenette, tore open the fridge, and fumbled for his cook set. After today, he wouldn't have to hide his habit from anyone. *Fuck 'em.* This was going to be his big day, liberation day, no more hiding, or worrying about being discovered. If he did this right, he would be on his way to Sao Paolo by this time tomorrow and Estados Unidos could kiss his ass goodbye.

He took his lace up boots and socks off and inspected his feet. The bottom of the left foot at one time was pink but now it was yellow and jaundiced with pus swollen needle pricks making a path up from his toes to the arch. He snapped the rubber tube around his ankle and flexed his toes to get the veins to stand out, spotted a couple that looked promising, then focused on his speedball. His big hairy baboon, his addiction, was getting bigger with each day, its big red ass riding on his shoulder, screaming insanely with a death head grin on its snout. Until recently, he could get by with blow during the day, just as long as he could ride the horse at night. Now, he needed to mix heroin and coke just to maintain some degree of stability. He didn't hit for pleasure anymore. Now, it was a deep need that tore him apart, if it wasn't managed. If he didn't track-up at least three times a day now, he would start bouncing like those freaks that live in the bushes down at the Truman Annex.

Under the heat of the lighter's flame, the powder and crystals began to melt into a swirling vanilla and brown viscous syrup, then into a cloudy yellow fluid that reminded Coltier of bees' honey. He deftly one-handed the needle into the liquid and sucked it up into the syringe, flicked the tube with his forefinger a couple of times to get the air bubbles to separate. Satisfied that all was ready, he slapped the target area and jabbed the needle into a thin blue vein. *Houston, we have liftoff.* The anticipation was there, knowing that the world would change in an instant. He watched the amber magic enter his vein as he pushed the plunger down slowly, loving this split-second before the spitball hit his system and exploded. It was like a void between life and death where he could taste and smell ozone burning in the air. Then, a huge nova of bright colors slammed his brain and he slumped back in the chair, a sensation akin to an out-of-body experience shook him, before he slumped forward to the floor, flying through the universe.

After an hour floated by, Coltier came back to earth, slowly, as waves of consciousness washed over him. He sat up, rubbing his face, unaware of how much time he had been under, but knew it couldn't have been too long. It was still light outside which reminded him of what he had to do and to prepare for what was coming. His heart skipped a beat, when he thought about what lay ahead. He would have to be on his toes and think everything through completely. Otherwise, it could cost him his life. No one in his right mind would do what he was going to do, but, he knew the information he had would insure his survival.

Coltier pushed up off the floor and ran cold water over his head in the sink to clear the purple haze that surrounded everything he looked at. The sensation of power and cunning, magnified by the opiate running through his system, gave him confidence in his plan to blackmail Marcel Duvalier. It was just a question of how much he was going to ask for, in exchange for the account number he had gotten off the Rover's dashboard. He was a hundred percent sure that this number was what Little Doc was after, and that Marsh and the woman were side issues to be dealt with at his leisure.

Coltier stuffed a chocolate bar in his mouth and ate it hungrily, then, chewed a second one, slowly, as he dialed a number from memory.

"Yes," a seductive voice said.

"This is Bolivar calling for Monsieur Duvalier."

"A moment please, Monsieur," music played softly on the line.

"This is good news you have for your benefactor, isn't it, Coltier?" Marcel asked, without a greeting or preamble.

A sudden wave of fear raced through Coltier's body, as the enormity of the risk he was about to take smacked him in the gut.

"Uh, yes, Monsieur, I think I may have what you seek," he said. "I have done what you asked of me, *Poppy*. I must tell you it, was obtained at a terrible cost to us. Paul LeClerc and his men were killed, in the process of obtaining it. They fought gallantly but were cut down by that devil Marsh..."

"LeClerc is dead? How could that be? He would never place himself in a position to be killed. The man was a coward. He would have run away, at the first sign of harm to himself."

"It was all very confusing, *Poppy*. The entire fight lasted only a few moments. I had just beaten the information you seek out of Marsh when, somehow, he had worked his hands loose, grabbed a pistol from one of the men, and started shooting. The man is crazy, *Poppy,* even though I shot and wounded him, he still managed to escape."

"So, tell me, Bolivar, why is it that you are still alive, if Marsh is so crazy? Why didn't he kill you too?" Marcel questioned.

"*Gris-gris*, *Poppy*. My life is charmed, Monsieur. My *Loa* is the spirit of life. I will only die when I ask to die."

Just the mention of a man's personal *Loa,* or spirit guide was enough for Marcel to change the subject. It was not healthy to ask what goes on between a follower and his guide. Ask the wrong question and a *Kami* spirit could come in the night and steal your soul, leaving you *zombie.*

"Never mind that, just give me the information Marsh gave to you."

"Yes, well that is the problem, *Poppy.* I cannot just give it to you, you see. I need something in return…"

Coltier could feel Marcel's anger even before the words traveled across cyberspace. When the words arrived, he had to hold the phone away from his ear.

"*Something in return*! You thief, you murderer, son of a party boy, you peasant. I will kill you with my own hands, I will gouge your eyes out…" Marcel paused for breath.

Coltier could hear Marcel struggling to catch his breath and thought he had better make his case quickly. "*Poppy*, relax, I do not want much. Just consider all the good things I have done for you and your father over the years. You are my island family, your father is my father, and we are like brothers…"

"How dare you compare yourself to a Duvalier. You are from scum and you will die as scum. I will see to it that your bones are scattered on the garbage dump you came from, Bolivar. You have tried to blackmail the wrong man. I will ask you once more for the information. If you do not give it to me, I will have you killed."

Coltier knew that this was not an idle threat and his plan had backfired. Any thought it would be easy to get anything out of this lunatic was crazy. "Marcel, I want three million dollars for the information. I want it in cash and I want it in my hand, before I give you the information. If you say no, then I will kill myself and you will never recover your treasure."

"You are so stupid, Bol. Go ahead and kill yourself, you fool. I'll track down Marsh and squeeze him until he tells me where it is," Marcel said, with venom in his voice.

"You are the fool, Marcel. Don't you think Marsh is already on his way to get his hands on your treasure? He is not going to sit on this information, not when he knows what is hidden, where it came from, and what your plans are for it."

"Marsh knows nothing. He stuck his nose into my business because of the whore, and I am going to kill him for causing me so much time. If he had stayed out of it, I would have the information from the woman and would have the treasure in my hands by now. But no, he has taken the woman from me, killed my men, tried to kill me, and so, now, I owe him a slow torturous death," Marcel said.

The line went quiet as Coltier thought fast.

"But *Poppy*, what if you are wrong? What if Marsh is on his way right this moment to recover your father's money." This was a wild guess, but he knew his time was just about up. "Your father will hold you responsible for his loss. You and I know what he would do to you if it was you who cost him the presidency…" he let his voice trail off, holding his breath.

Coltier pulled the phone from his ear as loud shouting and banging rolled down the line. He could hear the incoherent screams of rage and the crashing of dishes and furniture. This went on for several minutes and then there was quiet. Coltier held the phone tightly to his ear, trying to pick up the slightest hint of what was going on. The silence was lethal. He knew that the next words would condemn him to death. He had overreached, he had fucked up, he was a dead man.

"Bol, listen. I have given it some thought and I would like to suggest two million, instead of three. I just can't put my hands on three this time of day, but two should be no problem," Marcel said, in a normal rational tone.

Coltier was immediately alert for trouble. Although he knew of Marcel's swings from sanity to insanity had cost men their lives, he was not going to be taken in so easily.

"Thank you, *Poppy*. Your counter offer is quite generous and I accept it. My only demand is that it be in cash and that I receive it today. Is this agreeable?" His heart was jack-hammering an irregular beat while he waited for the answer.

"Oh, Bolivar, how I have underestimated you, my friend. You are, indeed, a tough negotiator. I will go along with you, except I have a demand myself. Would you like to hear it?"

"Yes, of course, Marcel. Whatever you ask, if it is possible, I will grant it."

"This is my demand. When I give you the two million dollars, you give me all the information that you obtained from Marsh...and, you must tell me where he and the whore are hiding. Without that information, the deal is off."

"But, I don't have any idea where they are. They could be any place."

"That is my offer, Bol. Take it or leave it."

Coltier felt himself being boxed in. He knew that if he refused, he would be dead before the day was over. He also knew that Marcel would make it as painful as possible. He wasn't sure he could deliver on Marsh, but now, he had no choice. He had to go along with Marcel and just think smart and hope he could pick up Marsh's trail. As a last resort, he knew he could draw down on Marcel and his henchmen and kill them before they got him. *Hell, yeah, if Marcel wants to play for keeps, I can too.*

"Ok Marcel, we have a deal. You give me two million dollars and I'll give you the account information, Marsh, and the woman."

"Bol, I'll be at your trailer at 8:00 p.m. Don't fail me."

"I'll be here. You too, *Poppy*, don't fail me."

Chapter 26

The Forbes twins, Otis and Orin, owned the Keys National Bank located on Duval and Greene Street, a few blocks down from the Sand Bar. The bank had been in the Forbes family for four generations, founded by Major Cletus Forbes after the War Between the States ended. Old Cletus was running hard at war's end carrying two saddlebags filled with gold taken from the Army's paymaster destined for Mobile. He rode hard and fast until he couldn't go any further unless he wanted to sail down to Cuba. He set up a small real estate and loan sharking business in Key West and loaned money to the local turtle harvesters, the dozens of shipwreck salvagers, Negro fishermen, and Greek spongers. He was tightfisted and a shrewd businessman, and soon, turned his stolen gold into a family fortune. His sons took over the business after him and doubled the family fortune on bootleg booze, usury loans, and real estate. The business changed with the times over the years and continued to make money. When the local waters had given up their last sponge and turtle oil went out of fashion back east, and sailing ships gave way to steamers with better navigation charts and methods, the family followed the money and became legitimate bankers. Making money was in the Forbes DNA and they soon became the dominant Conch family in Key West. The Conch families had become wealthy off the backs of lesser men and their misfortunes over the years. Misfortunes like embezzlement, theft, intimidation, fires, lynchings, and many unsolved disappearances. With each misfortune, a Forbes could be found profiting, somehow.

The twins carried on the family tradition of squeezing a profit out of a grain of sand, crying foul all the while. To the brothers, there was no such thing as white-collar crime or business ethics. The business of business was to make money, losers set up rules and laws to make them competitive. The Forbes boys were businessmen and played by their own rules.

So, when short roly-poly Otis greeted Jack Marsh in the lobby of the bank with a handshake and several friendly slaps on the back, all the tellers knew that the day would be a good one for the bank.

"Jack, by God, boy, where have you been?"

"I'm sorry Otis. I didn't have time to change..."

"Change? I don't care how you look, I'm talking about not seeing you for the longest time," he said, and quickly ushered him into his private elevator that took them up to his plush private suite of offices.

Inside the elevator, Otis couldn't contain his glee. "What is it this time Jack? Gold bars, drugs, state secrets, maybe nubile young native girls...hmmm?" Otis's eyebrows bounced up and down in anticipation. "By God, I wish I was young again and in the middle of things like you. Just imagine, Jack, if we could have been partners together. By God, we would own the Caribbean and half of Central America."

The elevator door slipped open silently onto a wood-paneled outer office where a gorgeous brunette sat primly at a clear glass desk. As strung out as Jack was, he paused a moment to appreciate the woman.

"Have you met Dixie, Jack? She is Marie's replacement. Been here a few weeks, right, Dix?"

"Yes, Sir, Mr. Forbes, if you say so," she said coyly.

"Dix, Dear, bring us in a couple of coffees when you get the chance, Honey."

"Yes, Sir, Mr. Forbes, two coffees."

Dixie placed the mugs of coffee on the large desk, giggled as she minced across the thick carpet, and closed the door behind her.

"Best piece of quiche I've ever had, Jack," Otis said to the closed door. A few heartbeats skipped by, and he sighed. "OK, spill it, what do we have? Start at the beginning. I want to hear it all start to finish, don't leave anything out."

Twenty minutes later Otis sat back in his plush chair and let his breath out. "Jack, you never disappoint. What a charmed life you live! I have never seen any other man that can fall into a bucket of slops and come out with a fistful of dollars like you can," he said, appreciatively. "But, this one is going to get your throat slit, if we don't play it right. The Duvaliers have been a plague throughout the Caribbean for decades, and this Little Doc character sounds like the reincarnation of his grandather. Let me tell you a quick story of the ruthlessness of the old man, Papa Doc. When he became President of Haiti back in the 1950's, the country was flat ass broke. The country did not have a dime. He approached my father to help bring U.S. business to the Island. My father, the old fool, loaned Duvalier two million dollars, in return for a percentage of all the business he brought to Haiti. My father spent months traveling the country, wooing businesses to Haiti. In the end, the only industry he managed to set up was baseball manufacturing..."

"Baseballs," Jack said, thinking he had not heard correctly.

"Yes, baseballs. Haiti became the world's largest manufacturer and exporter of baseballs, thanks to my father. Balls from Haiti were all the pro teams would use, except now, Taiwan has taken over the lead. To this day, we are still waiting for repayment of the two million dollars loaned to Papa Doc, and our share of the baseball business."

Otis offered Jack a cigar out of an old gnarled box, and sat back.

"But that's not the story I wanted to tell you. As times became more desperate for the country, old Papa Doc began selling his fellow citizens to the highest bidder around the world. A potential buyer would only have to make contact with a certain government department, state his requirements, and soon afterwards, a product would be delivered. He wooed homosexuals from around the world, promising promiscuity with handsome young men for almost nothing, just a small value added tax upon arrival and departure. The gay tourist business skyrocketed and remained the gay destination of choice for decades, up until the AIDS thing ruined it. By that time, however, half of the male population was diseased and physically ravished. To replace this loss of revenue, Papa Doc began supplying cadavers to medical schools around the world for research purposes. Medical schools in the U.S. became the largest recipients of these *specimens* of dead, but, surprisingly, youthful, male bodies. Fresh blood, also, became a huge export for the country. It seems that there was no end to donors, Jack. One might even say that some gave their all, in support of this government program."

"Unbelievable," Jack said, as he hung on the last words. "How is it we have never heard any of this? You would think that the news people would be all over a story like this. Can't we do something about it?"

"Business, Jack, business. Your response is a natural reaction that a compassionate person would have. To a businessperson however, it is capitalism in action." He laughed, slapping his desktop.

The door opened and Dixie appeared.

"Yes, Mr. Forbes, you rang?"

"Yes, yes, come in, Dixie," he motioned. "Be so kind as to make Mr. Marsh and me a toddy, would you, Dear?"

"Of course, Mr. Forbes, *anything* for you," she answered, with emphasis.

"Jack, what do you say to a splash of Southern Comfort over ice?"

"I'll pass. I still have a lot to do today, but I'll take a rain check."

"That's too bad, Mr. Marsh. Mr. Forbes says I make a wicked toddy. You sure you won't change your mind?" she asked, as she pushed a paneled wall that turned silently, revealing a stocked bar.

"I'm sure, Dixie, but thanks. Mr. Forbes and I are about to wrap this up and then I'll be out of your hair."

Dixie, unconsciously, ran her hand through her hair and with veiled seductive eyes said, "A rain check it is then."

"Ah…yes, yes…back to business," Otis said, having caught the innuendo tossed at Jack.

"So, Jack. What exactly is it you want me to do in this matter?"

"You have corresponding relations with the Bank of Cayman, right?"

"Of course, as we do with all major banks in the hemisphere. As you know, in most cases, we have a very close relationship with all the island banks that go well beyond the usual correspondence courtesy. I dare say, we are one big happy family."

"Then you shouldn't have any trouble in finding out how much is in this account and making it disappear somehow, right?" Jack had scribbled the account number and the words Cay Brac on a bank envelope as he had told the story to Otis.

"Jack, I was hoping this was where we were going with this. I am confident that, with your go-ahead, the account in question will be closed by end of business today. I would think our customary banker's transaction fee of twenty percent is acceptable to you, plus, the usual ten percent for yourself and ten each for both Orin and me. Considering the risk with such transactions, such an onerous fee is almost obligatory, wouldn't you agree?" Otis said, with a twinkle in his eye.

"That works for me, just like last time. But forget about my share. Take out twenty percent for Coco and set it up in some kind of trust fund, then, convert the rest to the most worthless currency in the Hemisphere..."

"That would be the HTG, the Haitian Gourde."

"Ok, then, convert it all to HTG," Jack laughed, at this turn of events. "When Marcel Duvalier finds that he is sitting on his own worthless money, he is going to go ballistic and that's when payback strikes."

"Yes, well, be that as it may, that is not a bank concern. The less we know about that end of the escapade the better. Right Jack? That is your end of the business. I'm just your friendly banker trying to make a buck," Otis said, covering his ears, then laughed.

"Oh, by-the-by, Jack. I would like to deduct what is owed the Forbes family from the booty, if you have no objection, bread upon the waters and all that, by God."

"Otis, take as much as you like. Let's just hope that old Grandmother Duvalier stashed U.S. Dollars and not Gourdes."

"No matter, we'll sell off as much as we need to make our profit, Jack. If it turns out that the coffers are empty, so be it, and justice would have been served, by God."

Chapter 27

The afternoon sun smacked Jack, as he took the bank's side exit onto Front Street and hurried toward Whitehead. In front of city hall, he snagged an empty park bench and sat. The shade from the ancient banyan tree did little to lower the heat. A couple of local kids were playing hide and seek among the dozens of secondary trunks that grew from the tree, oblivious to the heat and didn't pay any attention to him. Jack wiped the sweat from his face and dialed the number that he had been dreading. He had screwed up, royally, by not calling Bill Price the moment Coco had been abducted the other night. And now, after everything that had happened, Bill was going to go ballistic. Jack had been so intent on saving and protecting Coco and himself that he had let too much time slip by before making this call. AIC Price was head of the State's Bureau of Investigation in Miami. His office was tasked with major crimes, espionage, and terrorism that affected the state. Price had, also, spent twenty years in the Marine Corp, serving as Provost Marshall for all Marine Corp brigs. He was one tough s.o.b.

On the first ring, the phone was answered, "Florida State Bureau of Investigation, how may I direct your call?"

"Agent-In-Charge Price, please."

"May I ask your name and the nature of your call?"

"I'm a friend. Tell him Jack Marsh is calling."

After a couple of minutes, a gruff voice mumbled, "Jack, I'm in a meeting. I'll have to bounce back to…"

"It's about Coco, Bill. We need to talk now."

"*Coco*! What's wrong? Has something happened to her?"

Jack could almost see the big black face of his friend struggle with alarm and apprehension and knew that this conversation was not going to go well.

"It's a long story that's going to take a few minutes, Bill..."

"Is she alive? Just tell me that," he demanded

"Yes, she's alive and safe...for now," Jack said, feeling guilty.

Jack could hear a loud rush of exhaled air.

"Thank God! How bad is she hurt?"

"Well, a mild concussion, a broken jaw, probably two or maybe three ribs fractured, some major bruising..."

"Damn, what hit her, a dump truck?"

"Uh, no, Bill, she wasn't in an accident. She was kidnapped and beat up pretty bad by her captors...."

"*Kidnapped*! Who kidnapped her? Give me his name, he's a dead man..."

"Bill, calm down. I need to tell you the whole story, and then we need to figure out what to do next.

Just sit back and listen to me," Jack said, and began relating the details of the last three days.

"You mean to tell me that all of that has happened in the last thirty-six hours, and *this* is the first I've heard of it? Never mind that, Coco and I are engaged to be married and I'm going to break your fucking neck for not calling me. Never mind that. What I'm saying is that you and your boys go riding up to Little Haiti and shoot up the place. You killed an unknown number of people, broke into a foreign consulate, shot up *that* place, leaving more killed and wounded behind. Then, you haul ass to Key West and have another shootout with some Haitian Tonton Macoute thugs. There's a rogue Deputy Sheriff trying to get his hands on you, and now you're on the run, maybe leaving the country," Captain Price said. "Did I miss anything?"

Jack knew Price was furious, by the sarcasm in his voice, as he recited all the details back to him. The only thing he held back on was the details of his meeting with Otis Forbes and their plan to wipe out the Cayman bank account before Marcel or any of his thugs knew about it.

"Uh, well, we did free Coco, and she's safe now…sort of."

"Jack, believe me, if Coco had been killed in all this heroic bullshit you pulled, I would kill you myself." He paused to let that sink in. "You live a charmed life, you're luckier than an alley cat, but, this might be your downfall. If you survive the ass-whipping I'm going to give you, then you have Marcel Duvalier on your trail, and he's like a pit-bull. He never quits the hunt...."

Jack was suddenly steaming with anger. He had laid back long enough playing nice guy, trying to play patty cakes with the bad guys and not hurt them too bad, trying to rationalize and play everything as if it were just a rescue mission. This game was far from over. Listening to Bill threaten him for what he had done over the last few days as if he were some loose cannon just threw gas on the fire. He was disgusted with himself. Yeah, he had played rough with the Tonton thugs, and wasn't even that upset when Marcel slipped out of his grip in the consulate's basement. He admitted to himself that he had proceeded with a half plan, a plan that rescued Coco. Save her, and life would go back to normal. He had misjudged his enemy. They were at war, and victory to them was to get the money that would put Marcel's father back in power and in control of an entire country. Coco was just a pawn, a pawn not even of her own making, not even known to her. She was placed in the game, even before she was born. Her grandmother was the game's grand mistress that started the clock ticking when she stashed the money in the Caymans, knowing that someday, a Duvalier would need it to reclaim the family's rule over the Island. She did not hide the money for her daughter to live happily ever after in exile. She meant all along for it to go to one of her male offspring. However, she hated her son, Jean Claude, 'Baby Doc', because he was not as strong or ruthless as his father, 'Papa Doc'. She knew that her whimpering son would squander the opportunity to set up a dynasty. No, she needed someone who wanted power so badly that he would kill anyone for it. If only she had lived to see her grandson, Marcel, 'Little Doc', the very image of the type of man she sought, as capable of killing his way to power and keeping it.

Jack knew the only way this was going to end was with Marcel dead and all tracks leading back to Coco and him. The problem was, he did not know how far Marcel's arm reached into the sheriff's office. He knew that Coltier was rotten, but was not sure about Sheriff Taylor. Taylor hated Jack because of past jurisdictional issues where agencies higher up the food chain protected him.

Jack needed Bill Price to give him cover with the Haitians. He knew that to take a fall on a capital crime, or not, was a razor thin line, defined by perception and clarity, usually, determined by the investigators. He needed to convince Price that his actions were the result of trying to do the right thing. He needed cover against the Haitians, on all the action to rescue Coco. He would worry about how to explain Marcel, once he finished with him.

"Bill, you listen to me, Buddy. You are my friend, but do not give me all that righteous bullshit about killing me *if* I had let anything happen to Coco. Coco is my family. I will do anything to protect her, and I did. Yes, I killed men to save her. I would do it again in a heartbeat, and I would do it twice as hard. Nobody threatens my people or me. As for 'Little Doc', he is dead meat. I have plans for that boy that would make Jeffrey Dahmer faint. Now, if you want to fuck around, wasting time, telling me what you're going to do to me, then this conversation is over. If you want to help me protect Coco, then quit with all the macho bullshit, and let's figure out how we are going to get her out of this mess."

The other end of the phone went silent for a few moments, as Price digested what he had heard. He knew that his threats against Jack were not real. He respected Marsh and considered him a close friend. The news of Coco being hurt caught him off guard. He just lost his head and took it out on Jack.

"Ok, Jack, I want you to tell me everything again, slowly, and don't hold anything back. If I'm going to save your ass…again, then I'll need to know it all."

It took longer with the second telling, because of all the questions Price asked. Jack kept the information to himself about the money in the Caymans. He told Bill everything, starting from Madam Duvalier hoarding money in a hidden account somewhere, that Coco's mother knew the secret location, but then, took the secret to her watery grave, somewhere off the Bahama Trench.

Price liked Jack's plan about taking his crew out on the blue and drop off the grid for a few days until everything shook out.

"Jack, I like your plan. In fact, if I'm to clean up this mess, then I need you gone. As soon as we get off the phone, I'll start getting things in motion. Meanwhile, load everyone up and hunker down off the Tortuga's, someplace where I can reach you. Once I have things under control, I'll shoot you a message that it's safe to come back."

"Chief Drummond has us anchoring off Moon Key, initially. There won't be any problem with comms. We'll stay there, until we hear from you," Jack said, as he let out his breath and sat back on the bench. He knew that Bill Price would cover his tracks…once again.

"Jack, I'm doing this for Coco," leaving unsaid that he was not going out on a limb again for Jack. This was the last time he was going to put his career on the line to cover for him.

Jack felt a chunk of their friendship disappear. But what was he to have done? Let Coco be tortured and killed because of some psycho lunatic? No, he knew he had done the right thing and Bill would come around, once he heard Coco's side of things.

"I understand, Bill. I'll be waiting for your call," he said, then hung up.

The two kids were sitting under the tree, fagged out from their game of tag. Jack called them over to him,

"Ya'll want to earn a dollar?"

"A dollar? What we got to do?" Both boys looked at each other, suspiciously.

"You know where the Sand Bar is on Duval?"

"Well, sure. We steal lots of aluminum cans from behind the place. That Mr. Cookie, he's a mean dude. He caught us one time and dusted us up good. We didn't go back for a couple of weeks after that. What you want us to do?"

Jack wrote a list of things on the back of Otis Forbes's business card he had stuck in his pocket. The list included his sat-phone, his Berretta 9 mm and ammo, and ten grand cash.

"I want you to go around back to the kitchen and ask for Mr. Lamont. When he comes, you give him this card and tell him this is from Jack. OK?"

"That will cost you two dollars, Mister. If we have to go to the backdoor, that Mr. Cookie is going to dust us up again. A dollar ain't worth a dusting."

"OK, two dollars, and tell Mr. Lamont I said to fix you boys a couple of grouper sandwichs with some french-fries and a cold drink."

"We on it, Bro," the taller one said, with a big toothy grin.

"Tell him to bring everything to the *Queen*. Can you guys handle all that?"

"Hell, yeah, we can do it." They turned and were gone in a cloud of dust.

Chapter 28

Jack let go of the jumper lines, then moved forward to toss the bowline onto the dock, as Chief Drummond eased the *Queen* away from the pier. The *Queen* slipped by the Oyster House on the port side and out into the harbor, sliding by rows of pleasure craft, dive boats, and million-dollar sport fishing craft. Flotsam, from the storm, would eventually sink to the bottom or be skimmed up by the harbormaster's cleanup crew. Gulls swooped down looking for a handout, then just as quickly cartwheeled away empty-handed, screaming out obscenities.

Chief cut through the outer anchorage like the pro he was, dodging anchored-up sailboats of every size and origin. Key West was an excellent place to layup during hurricane season, or to rest up after months of sailing the circle around the Caribbean Sea. It was, also, a good place to find work for a couple of months, long enough to save up a few bucks, then get back out on the water. Jack compared these people to the Old West, where a cowboy would ride into town, stay a few days, drink up his poke, and then, move on. It was the same for these wanderers, except their steed was a boat.

Once clear of the anchorage, Chief kicked up the twin diesel engines. The *Queen* answered and was soon up on plane, skimming across the gimlet clear water. Jack was sitting with his legs spread, hanging them over the bow, riding the long loping wave action like a Plains Indian on horseback. The wind and spray splattered his face as he breathed in deep, letting the fatigue and danger of the past few days' flow away. The relief he felt, after telling Bill Price everything and knowing that Bill would take care of it from here out, was a huge weight lifted off his shoulders. Just knowing Bill would square things with all the right people made up for the harsh words they had spoken to each other. Jack knew that he owed Bill big time, after this.

He pushed the last few days with the dead and injured aside, focusing on the hot sun on his back and the salty sea air. Jack smiled to himself at the memory of Otis Forbes hurrying him out of his office, all the while keeping his beady little eyes on his Girl Friday. It was

Jack's guess that Otis had his pants down around his ankles before the elevator hit the ground floor. *"I guess money can buy handsome,"* he said to the wind. See note below

"What was that, Jack?" Laura slid in close, circling her arms around him.

Jack turned and saw the long brown hair blowing in the wind and the deepest green eyes he had ever seen, eyes that shifted color with the changing sea. Laura had changed into a pair of baggy cargo shorts and an oversized t-shirt that she dug out of a locker in the crew's deck below and looked stunning.

"Do you think I am handsome?" he said, turning his face left and right, chin jutting out.

Laura peered closely, and said, "Mmm, no, I wouldn't call you handsome. Let me study your face," gazing at him, placing her hands on each cheek. "Nice dark hair, thick eyebrows, long lashes…broken nose leaning to starboard, scar on corner of mouth, scar on cheek," she said, pulling his shirt over his head to continue her exam. "One…two puncture wound scars on chest and abdomen…" Above, before he had no shirt on????

"I asked Laura Summers if I was handsome. I didn't ask Dr. Summers for a physical. Am I handsome or no? Before you answer, you need to know that I am also rich," he said, leering.

"Oh yeah? Rich huh? That's different. Sure, then you're not only handsome, you are, also, beautiful. My guess is that the girls can't keep their hands off you, and you accommodate them. Is this right?"

"It's a curse, Laura. I have had to live with it all my life. Women are my downfall. My life is one constant battle to break free of all the women…"

Laura laughed and swatted Jack playfully. "Well, that's going to stop, as of right this minute. If I'm going to be your girl, I don't want any competition, Mister. Do you get it? I don't share my men."

Jack wrapped his arms around Laura and pulled her to him. "I'm your man, Laura. You've got me," he whispered. "There'll be a lot of broken hearts around Old Town, but…," he added, playfully.

Laura pushed him away. "Men! You're alike, all of you, Jack Marsh. You want the truth. I'll give you the truth. You're not handsome. I'll bet you're not even rich. Do you think that's all women look for, good looks and money?" she said, scolding him. "I'll tell you why I love you. You're the most exciting man I have ever met. There's an aura of danger and intrigue surrounding you. Just below that thin veneer of civility is a cunning animal ready to pounce. You're filled with some kind of restlessness looking for something that, probably, doesn't exist, something out on the edge, something life threatening, and you'll never be happy until you find it. It's, probably, going to be the death of you." Laura threw her arms around Jack's neck, suddenly crying, and hugged him hard.

Jack rocked Laura gently while she cried herself out. He lay back on the deck cushion, pulling her with him, and let her whimper herself to sleep, holding her tightly.

The change in the engine pitch and the *Queen* dropping down off plane woke Jack up. The sun was a blowtorch hanging in a metallic blue sky. The water and sky merged into the same blue, off on the horizon. A small island of green seemed to shimmy in midair, like a desert oasis off the port bow, one minute suspended in midair, the next anchored to a lighter pool of blue from a kite string of horizon

"Stand by to let go the anchor," Bull's voice came over the mc2.

Jack and Laura scooted out of the way, as the windless started up and fed out the anchor line. Jack watched, as the shovel-nosed anchor hit bottom thirty feet down, then dug into the sandy bottom. He gave Chief thumbs up, took off his shirt, dove over the side, and followed the nylon line down to the bottom. On the bottom, he gave the line a good pull to set the anchor from slipping. Satisfied that they had a good hold on the bottom, he rubbed his arms and chest against the chill of the water sending goose bumps up and down his arms. He ran his fingers over his scalp where the gash had been just a few days ago. Now, there wasn't anything there. Whatever hoodoo ointment Mama Dey had used, it did the trick. Jack squeezed and probed the area with his fingers as he pushed off the bottom. Windless wench? SHIRT?

"Come on in," he yelled, as he broke the surface. "I'll race you to the island."

"You're on, Sport," Laura yelled back, and dove in.

Chief had anchored in the center of the small bay formed by a crescent-shaped coral and sand island called Moon Key. The Key was located on the western end of the Dry Tortugas, a small chain of coral atolls that lay forty miles off Key West. Moon Key was uninhabited and isolated, a good place to lay up for a few days, not having to worry about the daily hordes crowded on dive boats that stuck close to Fort Jefferson, ten miles to the south. Chief Drummond had chosen this particular Key to pull their R&R because he would be able to spot any incoming craft, night or day, with the *Queens* radar. He would set up a night watch schedule between Jack, Max, and himself, just in case someone got through the electronics and made it to the Key and out to the boat. There was no sense taking chances, especially with these Tonton crazies.

Jack struggled out of the water, winded, and flopped down next to Laura. Laura had beat him to the beach by a couple of minutes, had taken her t-shirt off, and sat sunning in her bra.

"That's not fair, you're sitting there all beautiful and luscious, and I'm too winded to do anything about it," Jack sputtered.

"Haven't you ever seen a woman in a bikini top, Jack?" she teased. "Pull those horns in and catch your breath. Then, we're going exploring."

Moon Key was a half mile from crescent tip to crescent tip, an atoll of white powdery sand, coconut palms, tropical underbrush, and small amphibious creatures and birds. The birds were colorful and plentiful. They summered on Moon Key and flew south to Columbia and Venezuela for the winter. How they knew it was winter in the Keys was anyone's guess, but they knew. The lee side of the key formed by the crescent horns embraced the lagoon of crystal-clear water rich with sea life. From the shoreline, the sugary sand bottom tapered off gradually for the first twenty yards, then dropped off quickly to twenty, then thirty feet. Plenty of water under the keel for the *Queen* to swing on the anchor line safely.

Jack led Laura down a single file path that led to the windward side of the island. The path wandered through thick stands of palm trees shrouded with ropey vines that hid hundreds of bird nests. Flashes of green, red, orange, and purple flitted from one nest to another, chirping wildly, in some song of life. Laura tweeted a few times, and soon had several birds on her head and shoulders, greeting their new friend with whistle-like chirps. The fun lasted a couple of minutes until one bird decided that Laura's hair would make a good nest and began to pull strands of hair from her head. Jack grabbed Laura's hand and began to run, as she pulled the little creatures out and tossed them in the air. In no time, they were back on the beach and in the water laughing and splashing each other. Jack grabbed her by the waist and pulled her into deeper water, squeezing her in tight to him. Laura wrapped her arms around Jack's shoulders, pulling his face to her and stared deep into his eyes. Some secret of nature took over and they were kissing, passionately, as their need for each other took over. Suddenly, they couldn't get enough of each other and clung tighter, touching, feeling, exploring. Jack, finally, had to push her away and swim to the surface for air, Laura was right behind him. They came up gasping for air and reached out for each other again.

"Jack…Jack," Henrí called, as he swung the *Queen's* rubber dinghy toward them.

"Damn, bad timing," Jack said, as he spotted Henrí waving.

"Double damn," Laura said adjusting her bra.

"We'll pick up where we left off later, just keep thinking dirty thoughts," Jack said, mischievously.

"You're on, big boy," Laura said, as she pulled away.

"Jack, Max said to fetch y'all. Dinner's ready."

The main cabin was crowded, everyone sat around the mess table, eating their first big meal in days. Max was busy spooning food on plates, limping around the table, encouraging everyone to eat up.

"You got your corned beef hash, your scrambled eggs, and your bacon. We've got cornbread, jams, and jellies, hot coffee and juice. All right, off Riker's main dining hall menu. Eat up, we got plenty…"

"Max, this is delicious! Where did you learn to cook like this?" Laura asked.

"It's a long story, Doll, but to keep it short, I learned how to cook at Riker's, when I was doing a six-year bounce for…never mind for what. They sent me there, while I was waiting for my lawyer to appeal the case. It was all bull, and the D.A. knew it. He needed a patsy for some burglaries on the upper eastside, so, he throws a net over the Bowery and pulled in a bunch of little fish. I was the littlest one. So *Bingo!* I took the fall."

"That's the short version?" Laura sat, wide-eyed as she listened to his story. She had never met an ex-con before.

"Well, there was some, what the fancy people call extenuating circumstances to the case that kicked it up from an easy two to three-year stretch to a capital. All of a sudden, I'm facing the come-to-Jesus needle, for something I didn't do. Some big shot off Park Avenue got himself killed trying to save his wife's jewelry from some so-called short guy caught with his hand in the kitty."

"Oh, my! I'm not sure I want to hear any more. Maybe later."

"You never heard of Max the Mooch, famous second story man?" Jack started.

"Hey, watch your mouth. I did my time. I don't owe nobody nuthin.' I paid my dues. Big time, too, and don't you forget it. Now, we going to eat, or are we going to bust my balls over something that happened in my youth?"

Suddenly, Rooster started clapping and laughing, "Rooster likes that story. Same thing happened to the crazy dog on Road Runner TV."

"Hey, I don't need no comparisons from a kid with a name like Rooster. Now, shut up and eat…and it ain't a dog, it's a coyote. Get your facts straight, kid. All of you people, eat before it gets cold. I'm not cooking for a bunch of ingrates. Besides, Cookie sent over a gallon of ice cream and a can of chocolate syrup. So, get busy, if you want dessert."

A million stars lit the night sky overhead. Jack and Laura sat on the work deck. The Milky Way was an explosion of pixie dust thrown across the heavens. Shooting stars raced across the sky like roman candles, coming from somewhere out beyond the beyond. Satellites crisscrossed the sky from every direction, reporting every detail of what they saw to their masters, machines of deceit and secrecy, of man's lack of trust of his fellow man, to spy and report.

Everyone had pitched in after dinner, and helped clean up, with Max supervising every task while he sat writing out the next day's menu. Chief Drummond was back at his station on the bridge, watching and worrying over the boat's instruments, as captains have a wont to do. Baby loved to who is BABY???? wash dishes. He inspected each plastic plate and utensil for the slightest blemish, and ran everything through the wash again, if there was any doubt. Henrí was below with Coco, feeding her chicken broth through a straw, and spooning small dollops of ice cream to her lips.

The *Queen* floated calmly on her anchor, sitting in a pool of inky black, except for the soft green glow from the bridge. The breeze out of the east was cool and smelled of the sea. An occasional chirp, coming from the island and the splash made by a fish on the water, were the only sounds, except for the lapping of water on the hull.

Jack and Laura had spread a blanket, watching and counting stars. They held hands tightly, waiting for everyone to settle down for the night, anxious to pick up where they had left off. It was not to be. Soon Rooster came out with Coco, limping and moving slowly, at his side. He sat her on one side of the blanket and hurried below to bring pillows up to make her comfortable. Max and Henrí joined them, after a having a couple of after-dinner toddies, bringing the jug of brandy with them.

Maybe it was the night and the brandy, or maybe, the adrenaline burn- off from a three-day high, but, the conversations were low and soft, like a wake, where the living let go of the dead and then move on. As the Milky Way moved across the heavens, and the talk fell off, in whispered exhaustion, one by one, the small band of warriors and players drifted off to sleep, huddled around the communal blanket, feeling the safety in numbers.

Chapter 29

Five minutes after Bill Price had hung up talking to Jack Marsh, he was on the phone to the State's Attorney General in Tallahassee. Despite the fact that the love of his life was in peril, she was, also, right in the middle of one of the largest rip offs of charitable aid in history. It was no secret that billions of dollars in cash and aid was sent to Haiti, over the past few years, through the United Nations, and other donor nations throughout the Americas. Not the contributors, nor the Haitian officials, themselves, could account for much of that money. The government had always been corrupt and ripped off billions of dollars, when aid flowed in. The money never seemed to trickle down, though, to the people who needed it most, and yet, the money just kept flowing, with hundreds of millions of missing currencies.

The State Attorney General had set up a task force, in Miami, under A.I.C. Major Bill Price, to pick up the money trail that came back into the state from Haiti. Price's mandate was to arrest and prosecute the perpetrators and their U.S. accomplices. After many months of investigation, the case broke down into three major groups who were involved. The first was the current President of Haiti and his immediate cabinet of ministers who siphoned off directly from the national bank, which the government owned and controlled. That money vanished into secret accounts around the world. The second group was U.N officials, who took their cut under the table for pushing and voting for the fabricated need of such large sums of aid. These were the truly corrupt who used their political position and influence at the U.N. to get loans and aid approved, at the expense of starving nations across sub-Saharan Africa. It did not bother them, for one second, that thousands starved to death everyday from lack of the world caring.

The third group was organized crime syndicates that used threats and intimidation to collect surcharges and value-added taxes on foreign companies that brought goods and services into the destitute country. The primary syndicate to use this method was the Tonton Macoute, under Marcel 'Little Doc' Duvalier and his father, Jean Claude, known as 'Baby Doc'. The Duvaliers were notorious thieves of government money, had been for over a half-century of dictatorial government, and always, seemed to get away with it. The only one who was charged with a crime against the state was Jean Claude 'Baby Doc', but to escape prison, he went into self-exile in France, along with a, reported, seventy-five million dollars of stolen money.

Jean Claude enjoyed an idyllic and protected life in exile for twenty-five years, then, returned on a wave of support from the poor and underclass of Haiti, with the promise that he would clean up all the island's corruption. His campaign was, soon, broke and money was needed for payoffs, kickbacks, and bribery. His son, Marcel, whom he hated…and, feared, became his strongman and collector, but, there still, seemed, never to be enough cash to feed the political machine. The presidency was slipping through his hands.

Major Price knew the biographies of both men from memory. He knew the hatred the father had for the son, and the odd love, the son had for his father. There was no doubt in anyone's mind that Marcel was a sociopath who killed for the fun of it. His role as leader of the Tonton Macoute gave him many opportunities to do whatever he chose to do to his father's enemies. Now that Price had learned that Coco was in Marcel's sights, and that she was the key to a fortune in stolen money that Jean Claude needed, he knew, he had to move fast, before Marcel got his hands on her again. To himself, he thanked Jack Marsh for his dumb heroics to save Coco and was, secretly overjoyed, that she was currently safe, thanks to him. However, as long as Marcel was out there on the loose, no one was safe.

Chapter 30

It was dark, by the time Bill Price's SUV's black multi caravans pulled up in front of Sheriff Taylor's cinderbock home. He sat in the passenger seat, collecting his thoughts. The last few hours had been hectic, as he gathered search and arrest warrants, cleared jurisdictional concerns with Tallahassee, pulled his team together and put together a plan. Because they had twenty-four-hour surveillance on Marcel Duvalier, they knew that he was on his way to Key West along with four of his shooters. This news set off alarm bells in Price's mind and had him convinced that Marcel was moving in for the kill on Coco, Marsh, and the others.

Price gave the signal, stepped out of the lead SUV, and started for the front porch. Two men from the tail end of the SUV stepped out and hurried to catch up with him, as he knocked. Behind them sat the rest of the team in five other SUV's, packed with twenty agents dressed in black combat gear and ready for any contingency.

"Why, hello Bill! What a surprise, what's going on?" Sheriff Taylor asked, as he looked at his guest and the two men behind him. "What's with the SWAT gear? Castro finally decided to invade Key West?"

"Sheriff Taylor, I have authorization from the State's Attorney General to place you under protective custody for the duration of this operation…"

"What operation is that, Price? I haven't heard of any operation," Taylor butted in, stepping out on to the porch and got in Price's space. "If I don't know about any operation on my turf, then there ain't going to be one. Got it? Now, tell me what this is all about."

"We have it on good authority that one or more of your deputies are involved with a money-laundering scheme with foreign nationals. The problem that we have here, Sheriff, is that we don't know for sure if you are involved or not, so, we want to hold you, until we can clear up what we know."

"What the hell are you talking about? Are you accusing me of money laundering? I'm the sheriff of this county. By God, I'm no crook," he said, balling his fists in anger.

"Sheriff, we have a report that you neglected to pursue an abduction the other night that involved foreign nationals against a local woman named Coco Duvalier. Is that correct?"

"Coco Duvalier? That hot little black gal that works for Jack Marsh…"

Price's swing was a blur, as his fist connected with the Sheriff's nose, then connected the sheriff's groin with a knee, and a hard fist to the nose again until the Sheriff bent forward in pain.

"Zip this fucker up and throw him in the back of an SUV. We're taking him with us."

Chapter 31

The white Escalade was hitting 90 mph, roaring past Shrimp Road and was three miles closer to Key West before the driver realized his mistake and doubled back. Highway 1 was dangerous at any time of the day, with all the curves and soft shoulders that fell off into mangroves on both sides. But at night, it could be, especially, deadly, if you were not familiar with this area.

"Toby, Brother, you get me killed on this road, I'll kill you dead. Now, keep your mind on driving."

"How you going to do that, *Poppy*? If you get killed, how you are going to kill me?" Toby asked, bobbing his head in time to the music on the radio, a big toothy smile lighting up his face

"You just watch. Now slow down, here's our road."

Toby made the turn and came to a stop, as Marcel turned in his seat to face the men in back. The four men in the back seats were wide-eyed and alert. Each held a weapon, ready for instructions.

"Snake, you and Carl, you two get out and walk to the end of the road and hide in front of Coltier's trailer. Anyone come down that road looking suspicious, take them down…"

"You want us to shoot them? Won't someone call the police if we start shooting...?"

"If you would shut your fucking mouth and let me finish, maybe I'll tell you what to do," Marcel said, spraying the man with spittle as he talked. "Someone comes snooping, you cut their throat. You got your cane knives?"

Each man slipped small machetes out of their side scabbards and brandished the knives for Marcel's benefit.

"Good. Toby, you stay in the car with the motor running. Turn it around, so it is facing back to the highway, in case we have to move fast. Bull, you follow me in. When you get inside, do not sit down, just move over to the side and watch for trouble. Coltier's a big man, so, if he tries any hand-jive judo stuff, be ready. Randy, you follow us inside Bolivar's place carrying the suitcase. No matter what, do not open the suitcase unless I say so. Coltier thinks there is two million dollars inside, and I want him to keep thinking that, until I say to open it. When you open the case, make sure the lid is facing you and he can't see inside. Just reach in, grab that Uzi, and open up. Be sure, very sure, make sure, you do not hit me, when you pull that trigger. That trailer's not very wide and I will be sitting next to him. OK, we all clear?"

Snake and Carl disappeared into the inky dark, as Toby drove slowly down the only road leading in and out of the trailer park. At the end of the road, Coltier's trailer sat in a rectangle of darkness with the surrounding mangroves, nothing more than undefined blotches of shadow. The night was filled with unfamiliar sounds that made the hair on Marcel's neck stand out. He sat, breathing through his mouth, adding to the night's noise, as he worked all the angles. What was Bol up to? Why were all the lights out, was it a trap? It was said that Marcel had a third eye and could see through any ruse. He was, also, a survivor and never put himself in harm's way, if he could get someone else to go for him.

"Bull, sneak up to the porch and see what that devil is up to. If you see anything suspicious get back here, fast."

Bull was a very large man, but, moved as quiet as a cat. He moved through the shadows quickly and stood on tiptoes to peek into a window. He froze, when he felt cold steel touch the base of his skull and someone whisper.

"Tell Marcel to bring the money inside fast. I think we have visitors around, but I'm not for sure. Something just doesn't feel right. Tell him that we'll do this really quick and then it's every man for himself. Now, move it."

Coltier slipped through the front door into his living room, then turned to watch when three shadows ran across the yard and up the steps.

"Are you crazy? Why are you still here, if you think there is trouble? You should have called me. We could have set up another place to do our business." Marcel said.

"Shut up, and listen," Coltier said, peering out into the dark.

Something was not right. The mangrove creatures were sending out different sounds tonight, a few unfamiliar splashes came from the back of the house earlier that could have been a gator, but it did not sound right. Coltier was still buzzing from the high of the speedball, later, followed it with a couple of lines of coke. But, he was still alert and his antennas were up and pinging.

Marcel felt the danger, as well, and stepped farther back into the shadows.

"Did you tell anyone I was coming here?" Marcel croaked.

"Why would I do that? We both want the same thing," Coltier said. "Let's just get this over with…"

A shot was fired out-front, then another, and another. Marcel fell to the floor and crabbed his way over to Coltier.

"You set me up! Who's out there? Jamaicans…Cubans…?"

"You're crazy, Marcel. I didn't tell anyone. You're nothing to me anymore. Just give me my money and I'll tell you the account number…"

The shooting outside turned into a raging firefight that quickly swung towards the trailer. Dozens of rounds smacked through the trailer's thin walls causing havoc inside. Bull grabbed his chest, in a spray of blood. He stumbled to the front door, firing his pistol and fell back with half a dozen rounds chewing up his body. Marcel huddled behind the couch and fired through the window across the room. His eyes were huge and wild in his head, and his mouth locked open, in a gaping maw of hate.

Randy snapped open the suitcase, pulled the Uzi out, and ran out the door, raking the muzzle back and forth on full auto. His body was riddled with return fire. As he fell to the floor, three men in black SWAT gear tore through the door with machine guns blazing. Suddenly, a huge explosion rocked the trailer off its foundation, as a bullet tore into the outside propane tank, sending hot shrapnel and burning gas over the attacking force, trailer, and mangroves. The trailer was an inferno of flames, as Coltier snatched Marcel off the floor and raced to one end of the trailer. Inside a small closet, he kicked out a trapdoor, dropped down on all fours, and slid through, coming out on the backside of the trailer. He reached back in and yanked Marcel through the escape hatch, and half-carrying, half-pulling, he made for the mangroves.

Behind him, the trailer was engulfed in flames, as the aluminum and plastic melted from the intense heat. The gunfire had stopped when the explosion occurred. Several of the attackers ran covered in flames, insanely beating at the fire eating their bodies before falling in a blessed death. Explosions and ammo, cooking off in the trailer, made it dangerous to move around, so those who were unharmed remained hunkered down in safety.

Coltier was in stagnant water up to his chest with Marcel riding atop his shoulders. The vision of himself as a gargoyle, perched on the shoulders of Saint Christopher, made Marcel laugh crazily.

"Faster my gallant steed, faster," he croaked, as he dug his heels in and hung onto Coltier's ears. *"I will give you riches beyond your imagination for saving your Poppy. I will buy you a kiloton of pure joy to suck up your nose, my beloved. You have saved the heir to the throne..."* he cackled insanely.

"Shut up or I'll leave you behind. We're not safe yet." Coltier said, feeling his way through the brackish water ahead of him. The going was slow from all the sunken trees and debris, causing him to stumble and sink, coming up spluttering and spitting. He had an idea of where they could hide, safely, if he could make it through the mangroves. Coltier and his impish jockey continued through the snake and gator-infested quagmire slowly, stopping only to let a moccasin slither by, or to wait to verify if a log ahead was, indeed, a log or a gator. The larger the log, the more animated Marcel became, splashing water and daring it to attack. Coltier held his breath in fear, as he sidetracked, and backed away from several *logs,* not being sure if it was going to eat him or ignore him.

Back at the trailer, the heat and deadly chemical fumes from the melting inferno caused Bill Price and his men to fall back. Six of his men were unaccounted for and he hoped that some of them may had escaped the explosion, but he would not know until the fire was extinguished. Meanwhile, he had several of his men go from trailer to trailer, evacuating everyone that was at home. Sirens blared coming from the south and north, the volunteer fire departments from each Key responded to the alarm sent out. The fire quickly spread to neighboring trailers, jumping from one to the next, eating everything in its path.

A hazmat team from the Boca Chica Naval Airbase kept everyone away from the scene until after daylight when they could go in and assess the situation. Firefighting equipment from the base arrived around three in the morning to lay down fire retardant foam used in plane crashes, trying to stop the progress of the fire. Two thirds of the trailer park's trailers were burned or damaged. The good news was that everyone was accounted for among the residents.

By sun up, at 7:00 a.m., Price and his team scattered out looking for his six missing men. Agent Jenkins was on the far side of Coltier's trailer and was alive, but had lost a lot of blood during the night from a stomach wound. He had survived the fire by dragging himself into the mangrove's dirty water and lay submerged with just his nose sticking out. Two bodies were found with multiple gunshot wounds not far from the bullet riddled Escalade. A dead man sat slumped over the Escalade's steering wheel, surprisingly, with a smile on his face and a bullet hole in his forehead.

It took two hours of guesswork to put the body count inside the trailer at five dead. The heat from the fire had melted plastic into flesh, into aluminum, into more plastic until the five bodies were indiscernible from the wreckage. Price did not know if Marcel Duvalier was one of the dead or not, but, one of the lumps of plastic close to the front door could be him. It would take DNA testing to know for sure, but he felt confident it was him. A larger pile of smoldering material in the middle of the floor was, preliminarily, identified as Deputy Coltier. The remaining three piles were marked as missing members of his team.

At 3:00 in the afternoon, Price was exhausted. He sat in the SUV with his head back and eyes closed, pretending to sleep. He was satisfied that every base was covered and the necessary people notified in Tallahassee and Miami to cover everyone up and down the chain of command. He had held two press conferences with all the cable channels plus the mainstream people. Both went smoothly, with brief outlines of what had taken place, what had happened, and who was involved. The official story was that the State's Bureau of Investigation closed down a major Caribbean money laundering syndicate, names and nationalities of the dead would be released, pending identification and notification to the affected countries.

Price flipped open his phone and hit Jack's speed dial number. A half- minute lapsed before it rang. After several rings, the phone was answered.

"Captain Drummond speaking."

"Chief, it's Price, I need to speak with Jack."

"Wait one. He's over the side."

Price could hear the Chief yelling for Jack... "Jack, It's Bill Price on the line...hurry up!"

The phone emitted several muffled noises and then Coco was on the line.

"Dill, ith ee, Coco." She could barely talk, coherently.

"Coco, oh, Baby, it's so good to hear your voice..."

"Nee too. Dill, I love you." He felt her love for him through the phone.

"Take it easy, don't talk, and don't hurt your jaw. I'll see you in a few hours. Now, Baby, let me talk to Jack."

Jack spoke up, "Is this good news or bad news?"

"Good news, we got him and his mutts. Come on home," Price said, happily, feeling the fatigue roll off him.

"Got him, as in, dead got him, or cuffed got him?"

"Dead got him. Come on back to Key West and I'll fill you in. Just one thing though, you or your people are not to talk to any of the press or any law enforcement, got it? You do not know anything. You have never heard of any one named Marcel Duvalier or the Tonton Macoute. You open your mouth, I will send you to work on a road gang for ten years. Now, pull that anchor up and bring Coco to me."

Chapter 32

It was a little after eight when Chief Drummond pulled the *Queen* alongside the dock and cut her engines. Jack and Max made quick work of the bow and aft lines, and hurried back inside the main cabin to get out of the light rain. Two hours out of Key West, the sky had clouded over and a light rain kept everyone inside the main cabin. Morale was running high. Max put together a feast of fried fish, steaks, and delicious spiny lobsters that they pulled up from the waters around Moon Key. The meal was finished off with fruit cocktail, sugar cookies, and hot coffee. Laura had pretended to fall in love with Max, announced that she was taking him home with her, where he would cook for her and live in communal bliss forever and ever.

"I don't think so," Jack fired back. "Besides, its common knowledge that he has some incurable STD that even the Mayo Clinic couldn't cure…"

"That's a lie, Jack, and you know it. Herman Hospital in Houston spotted what it was, immediately, and stopped it, before it got any bigger," Max said, belligerently.

"Oh, my, too much information. I take back everything I said," Laura laughed.

Now, tied up alongside, the rejuvenated group began to shuffle around, gathering their belongings, tired and relied that their odyssey was at an end.

Bill Price called out as he swung aboard and swooped Coco up in his arms. They clung together for several minutes, crying and hugging in joy and relief. Coco was trying to talk, but could only get out a few muffled words. She finally gave up and just held on to her man.

"Who's that man squeezing Ms. Coco?" Rooster demanded, as he came up from the crew's quarters. "You stop this minute, or Rooster will hurt you. He promises," he threatened.

"Whoa, big fellow, I'm her friend. She's safe with me," Bill said.

"Ms. Coco is my job, not yours. Give her to me, I mean it," Rooster threatened, as he started towards the couple.

"Rooster, it's okay. Bill is our friend," Coco said, holding a hand up. "Come here and I'll introduce you to him."

As soon as Coco said that they were friends, Rooster's demeanor changed, and his face lit up in a huge grin. "Can he be Rooster's friend, too?"

Big macho Bill Price pulled one arm free of Coco and motioned for Rooster to come to him. A moment later, the three were hugging and crying, blubbering like long lost family members.

"Disgusting spectacle," Max moaned, sidestepping the three and went out on deck. "Jack, I'm taking off. I'll hoof it over to Sears Town and pick up my cab, if I can find it. God knows where Lamont parked the sumbitch. Probably took it for a frigging joy ride and left it on empty…frigging tires are probably bald too. I'll kick his ass when I see him."

"Be careful, Max. This mess is over, but, just in case, stay low. Call me if you have any problems," Jack said.

"Will do, Jackie," Max answered back, with a wave, as he pulled his collar up against the light rain.

"Say, Jack, Chief told me to ask you, can I stay aboard and help out for a few days until we see what's what? What do you think?" Henrí asked. "I'm in no hurry to get back up to Miami, seeing as there's really nothing left for me up there. That old house is nothing but bad memories filled with ghosts. I'm just not ready to deal with it, don't you see?"

Jack slapped the old man on the back. "Henrí, you stay aboard as long as you like. You're part of the family, now, and we need you around here. The *Queen* needs a lot of work, and I'm sure the Chief would welcome someone aboard he could boss around."

"Well, I'm kind of bossy my damn self, so we'll just have to see how that works out," the old man grinned. "But I do love a good spit shine and polish, and truth be told, I think I'm a better cook than old Max ever was," he laughed.

"Oh, Lord, don't say that around Max, there will be a murder for sure."

"Jack, take me home. I need to take a long hot bath, put on clean jammies, and sleep for about umpteen hours," Laura said.

Jack gave Laura a lascivious grin and a wink. "Give me a few more minutes with Bill, then we're off."

The few minutes turned into an hour, before Laura and Jack made it off the boat and caught a cab. Bill had recounted the events of the last twenty-four hours, while the group sat in silence, listening. It seemed that none of them would be identified being involved, thanks to Bill's efforts to cover their tracks. When Bill got to the part about the Cayman account having been closed and empty for over thirty years, Jack felt a sinking sensation. All the fighting and killing for what? Not even a dime for Coco, or anyone else. It had all been a lie.

"But, Bill, how can you be sure? I thought that Marcel was tasked by his father to find and take the fortune that Grandmother Duvalier stole years ago."

"Those were all rumors, and folklore, Jack. It never had been proved, one way or the other, that the old woman had actually stolen anything."

"But what about Coco's mother's diary and the secret account?" Laura asked.

"There was a record, our people found today, showing an account set up for Renee Duvalier, Coco's mother, but it had been emptied years ago by local relatives on Cayman Brac. There is not a dime, in any account in the Caymans."

The cabin fell silent, as everyone digested the news about the money.

"Well, at least, we're all alive," Jack said, forlornly. Even though his deal with Otis Forbes did not include any of the money for him, he still felt cheated, and a little pissed about no one getting anything. It had all been for nothing.

Laura and Jack were quiet in the taxi, as it cut across town. The swishing of the wipers was hypnotic, they held hands, lost in their own thoughts.

"Now what, Jack?" Laura asked.

"We move on, get all this behind us, and keep on with business as usual."

"What about us?"

Jack turned his head, slowly, looked at Laura and squeezed her hand tightly, "I'll show you 'what about us' in about ten minutes," he said as he bounced his eyebrows.

The cab pulled to the curb with a splash at Laura's house. Jack gave him ten bucks, hopped out, pulling Laura by the hand behind him, and ran for the porch. At the steps, he came to a sudden stop and pulled Laura to him.

"Shhh, hold it," he whispered. "I thought I saw a light go off."

Laura clung to Jack. "I turned off all the lights and locked the place up when I left, Jack."

"Look, there it goes again. Did you see that?"

"Yes, that's the door to my office. Oh, Jack, I'm scared. Someone is inside."

"Shhh, stay here. I'm going up on the porch and take a peek."

Jack hunched over, walked softly to the front door, and twisted the handle. The door gave off a squeak and opened an inch. Jack pulled it closed and tiptoed back to Laura.

"Someone is inside. I'm going to go in and find out who it is. You stay here."

"No way! I'm going too, Jack. You are not leaving me out here by myself."

Jack took her by the hand and went back to the street. "Go down to the widow's, and wait for me, I won't be long. It's, probably, just one of the homeless guys from the cemetery looking for loose change. Now go."

"I'll call the police from the widow's, Jack. Let's don't take any chances."

"No! No police. We don't want any local police sticking their nose into anything we're involved in. Didn't you hear what Bill said...no police? Now run."

Jack watched Laura turn into the widow's sidewalk, then waited a few minutes. The light had not reappeared, Jack watched and waited. He took a deep breath, let it out slowly, and turned the knob. Rain hitting the porch roof hid the squeaking noise of the door, as he opened it just wide enough to slip inside, then close it behind him. The coat rack standing in the corner of the foyer gave Jack a jolt, he pointed his pistol at it, waited, then moved on. Laura's house, that she had refurbished, was one of the old mansions built at the turn of the last century. The flooring was made using banyan tree planks that gave off a beautiful shine, but were loud, even when one was tiptoeing. Jack slid off his shoes and worked his way to the office door. A dim light shown from the crack at the bottom, but there was no noise coming from inside. Jack dropped to a knee and put one eye up to the old-fashioned keyhole. It took a moment for him to make out someone lying on the exam table, apparently sleeping.

Jack turned the knob and pushed, letting the door open as wide as it could go. He remained in the shadows and waited to see what the man would do. Jack recognized Deputy Coltier as he stared back at Jack through glassy unfocused eyes. Jack walked up to him, keeping his pistol pointed at his bare chest, ready for any sudden moves. As he got closer, the smell of sewage and noxious effluvia rolled off Coltier's body in waves. Jack gagged and covered his nose with his forearm. Coltier's arms, face and chest had deep cuts and scratches dug into the flesh, his bare feet were cut and torn. Jack surveyed the room quickly and understood what was going on. Laura's desk, cabinets, and drawers were ransacked. He spotted her medical bag, open and contents, dumped out on the floor; pills, bottles, bandages, and ointment tubes littered the floor around the bag.

Keeping a safe distance between him and the exam table, Jack moved around the other side and saw what he expected. A syringe, with at least three cc's still in the cylinder, was hanging from Coltier's arm with the needle still imbedded in his vein. Jack knew the junkies that worked the alleys around town called this hot tracking. The addict would fill a syringe with a speedball, shoot a cc or two, and then let the kit hang until the shooter wanted more. Someone who really wanted to stay loaded would do this, or someone with a death wish. Jack picked up an empty serum vial from the exam table and read the label, morphine. Another vial was on the floor, and a third was in Coltier's balled fist.

"Hey, Deputy, how they hanging, man?" Jack walked around the table so he could look into Coltier's face.

"Marsh, what ya doing...here," he said, still grinning. "You're supposed to be hiding from me..." he coughed and spluttered, as he laughed at his own joke.

"Well, there it is, my man," Jack said. "I guess we have this all fucked up...it's all turned around. You're supposed to be looking for me to kill me, and now look what we have. I'm standing here, thinking about killing you, and here you are, making it too damn easy for me."

Coltier started laughing, again, and tried to sit up, but couldn't make it. "I am so fucked, Marsh. I was on easy street...good job...good pay, not getting into too much trouble. Then, that frog Marcel comes hopping back into my life..." Coltier rubbed his eyes with his free arm, as if he were trying to wipe away a bad dream. "There's no going back for little Bol," he said.

"Where is Marcel? Is he here with you, in the house?"

"That freak is here, oh, yes, his body is here. But his fucking mind is gone...gone...gone," he mumbled, barely coherent. "I think I'm nodding, man...help me with the jab. I want it all...I want to go home, Marsh. I wanna...go...I can only die...if I ask my Loa...I want..."

Jack walked around to the other side of the table, keeping an eye on the door. Without really thinking about what he was doing, he snapped on a pair of exam gloves, pulled them tight, and stepped up to the table. Coltier was breathing in deep, then, exhaling slowly, two fingers on his left hand were twitching. Jack weighed the syringe gingerly in his hand, put his thumb on the plunger, and slowly pushed. Once the plunger bottomed out, he remained standing over Coltier.

"You're almost home, buddy. Let go, it's okay," Jack whispered.

It took less than a minute for the morphine hit to do its job. Coltier's breathing became shallow and less frequent until there was one last shudder, and then he was gone. Jack remained staring at what, until a moment ago, had been a man living with hopes, dreams, and a future. However, for some reason, he sought death and death answered. Jack did not know anything about the man and really did not care. He had, always, had the ability to close his mind to death and just accepted that he was different from most men. He did not know guilt or fear. If it became necessary to kill, he would not flinch from it, especially, if he felt justified doing it. There was a dead spot somewhere in his psyche that said, in matters of life and death, he was a law unto himself. He played by his rules, not humanity's.

The sound of someone singing broke the spell that held Jack. It was coming from upstairs. He pulled the syringe out of Coltier's arm and filled it from the vial in Coltier's dead hand, then wrapped it in a hand towel. He turned off the desk lamp, and tiptoed out into the hall. The singing was coming from upstairs, somewhere. Jack crept up the steps, taking his time, wanting to catch Marcel by surprise. He knew the man was fast, agile, and very dangerous. He knew that Coco or he would never be safe, if Marcel got away. This had to end tonight, and it could only end one way.

Jack peeked around the door leading to the bathroom and saw Marcel submerged in a bubble bath up to his huge head. Marcel saw Jack at the same time and let out a huge laugh.

"Ah-ha, I knew you would show up, sooner or later, Jack Marsh. I am glad that it is sooner. You and I have much to talk about, escape plans to make, money to find, Coco to fuck...hahahah."

Without any warning, Marcel was out of the tub running at Jack on all fours like a primate. He leapt up and smashed into Jack's chest, bowling him over. He continued, into the bedroom and jumped up on the bed. Jack was right behind him with his pistol aimed at the deformed body. Marcel stood balanced on the bed, weaving from side to side, grinning insanely.

"What's the matter, Jack? Never seen a freak before?"

Marcel's naked body was a torture of spindly deformed legs, hips that angled out to the sides, a chest wall, double the size needed and topped with the huge head with the round eyes and deformed mouth with a cleft lip. It was as if some evil god had taken bones, jumbled them up in a bag of skin, and named it Marcel.

"You are one ugly fucker, Marcel," Jack said, as he walked toward the bed.

"*You* cannot kill me, Mr. Marsh. Only *I* can kill me...," his gaze jerked upward, as he sucked in drool. "Do you hear that...do you... Someone is calling for me...can you hear him...*Father, you, miserable prick...*

HAHAHA...look what you and Mother made...a freak, a fucking freak!"

Marcel's eyes glazed over. His head cocked at an impossible angle, listening to something far off. He snorted loudly and spat. He broke wind loudly and fell on the floor rolling. Jack jumped back, as the mad man tumbled around the room, seemingly possessed. Jack saw his chance and jumped on the freak, getting him in a headlock. Without a thought, he jammed the needle into Marcel's temple, in the soft spot between the ear and the eye, and pushed the plunger. He held on, as Marcel bucked and fought, shouting and spitting. In just moments, he stopped thrashing about and laid still. Jack pushed the body away from him and struggled to his feet, breathing hard.

Jack stood, staring at the body for a few moments, then his mind jumped back to the present. He had to get the bodies out of Laura's house, before she saw them and went crazy. He could not let the police find them either. These two were on his dance card and he, sure as hell, didn't want to go down for killing a couple of roaches like these.

He wrapped Marcel in a sheet from the linen closet and threw him over his shoulder. He hurried out the front door into the rain and across the street into the cemetery. He wound his way through several rows, until he was deep among the aboveground tombs. He flopped the body down on the wet path next to a large double tomb that appeared to be ancient and timeworn. The marble was eaten by time and winds with hairline cracks that it made it settle off center a bit. Jack ran his fingers around the old plaster seal that crumbled under his probing fingers. He put his hands on the lid, dug his feet in, and pushed. The three-inch slab moved a nit of an inch, then slid freely, with a loud grating sound. Jack jumped back not knowing what to expect. Neither a corpse nor skeleton jumped out at him, nor bats skittered off into the darkness. He laughed at his own fear, bent, picked up Marcel and slid him over the edge of the tomb's maw, letting him settle among the dust and tatters of the old occupants.

As he ran back to get Coltier, he realized that he was shaking, uncontrollably. He laughed at himself, then thought of how Marcel had cackled, wildly, and he cut the laugh off in mid-guffaw. Back inside, he rolled Coltier off the exam table, onto a sheet spread on the floor. Coltier was too big to carry, so, he dragged him down the front steps and across the street. The sheet snagged on something and he bent to free it, just as a car cruised slowly down the street and stopped a few doors down from Laura's house. A car door opened and a woman jumped out laughing and yelling goodnight to the driver. A moment later, it was quiet again except for the pounding of his heart. Jack gave up on the sheet, and dragged Coltier by the hands the final fifty feet. It took all of his strength to lift the body up and over the lip and into the waiting tomb. Jack was breathing hard from the exertion, but leaned into the marble lid and set it back in place. He inspected his work, then slid down on his haunches, with his head resting on his arms. The rain ran cold rivulets down his back chilling him. His body trembled, his mind flashed kaleidoscopic images of the murders. Vomit filled his mouth, he spat and let the rain fill his mouth, and spat again.

The enormity of the evil he had done tried to take over his thoughts, but, he forced them to the background and concentrated on what he would need to do to cover his tracks. He could dwell on it later. But for now, he needed to beat feet.

Back in Laura's house, he gathered everything he could find that belonged to Marcel and Coltier, and placed it all in a plastic trash bag. He scrubbed and dried the bathtub until it shined, then remade the bed. The clinic was easy to tidy up and he was soon finished, except, for the medical bag, which he left as he had found it. His story to Laura was going to be that he walked in on a couple of junkies, fought with them, and finally chased them off. End of story

Chapter 33

The Sand Bar had standing room only, as the tourists and crowds filled every seat, table, and space, drinking, laughing, and having a swell time staying out of the sun's attempt to burn the town down. Jack thought he had never seen it this hot. Maybe in Iraq, but not here. This was America. How dare the sun? It wasn't supposed to get this hot in God's chosen land. He sat working a glass of whiskey-tinged crushed ice, more for the alcohol intake than the sharp ice daggers that froze his throat. NAOA reported it to be 105° now, and projected it to climb, as the day went by, possibly setting a state record. *Hoopty-Fucking-Doo.* Frankly, he didn't care if the streets melted or not. Business was good, the bar's air conditioning unit was pumping out frigid arctic air, his place was packed, and Johnny Boofey was rocking the house.

It had been three weeks since the big fire at the trailer park. The story of the conflagration had been told so many times that very few people, actually, had it straight about what really happened that night. The official report was placed at eleven dead with thirteen trailers destroyed. The Governor and the Attorney General toured the carnage for a photo op to show how tough they were on crime, especially, when international criminals were involved. The fact that they never announced, exactly, who those international criminals were, seemed not to bother anyone. It was never, clearly, reported that the two primary targets were not among the burned at the scene, but had been tagged as MIA and presumed dead. The theory was that the two primary suspects had escaped from the trailer only to perish in the mangrove swamps from wounds and/or were drowned. Since a search of the mangroves did not turn up anything, it was quickly assumed that alligators had eaten them. As the days went by, and the two did not surface, the gator assumption held true and became fact.

Jack smiled, inwardly, at this assumption of death and secretly wished it were true. The truth of what happened had cost him a big chunk of his heart and left him feeling empty. Laura had seen through his ruse about the two addicts that he had fought and chased off. Surprisingly, for not having been in the house to see what actually occurred, she was damned close as to how things unfolded.

"Jack, you're lying to me. They were here, were they not? They were in my house, waiting for us. I know it. I can feel it. Hell, I can smell it. It smells like a sewage plant in here…"

"Laura, I swear, I'm telling the truth. It was a couple of druggies after your supply."

"Then, explain this," she said, as she emptied the trash bag with the wet filthy clothes inside. Jack had placed it by the backdoor to dispose of, later.

"Those belonged to the burglars, Laura. I don't know why they stink so badly." Jack could feel his lie falling apart.

"Jack, why didn't you just call the police and let them handle it. Don't you see what you have done? How are you going to explain this away? Like you have done everything else, get your buddy, the State or whatever, to cover things up for you?" Laura was shouting and crying, as she moved from room to room.

"Laura, quiet down. You are wrong. You don't know what happened, and you don't need to know. Now back off."

Jack was surprised by Laura's reaction, and saw a side of her he had not seen before. To be fair, she was seeing a side of him that she did not know existed either. Maybe it was good that they were having this out now, get it all out in the open, and bare their dark sides and weaknesses to each other, now, rather than later.

"I can't deal with this, Jack. I'm a simple person. I don't understand you people, and I don't understand how you can be so callous and selfish…"

"Selfish! What are you talking about? What have I done that is selfish…and what do you mean by *you people*?"

"Look, just go, Jack. I need time to think. I'm not sure this is a good idea for you to stay…"

That had been three weeks ago, and Jack had not heard a word from Laura. He, desperately, wanted to call her, but every time he started to dial, he would cut it off. She needed to make the first move. The ball was in her court.

Jack eased off his stool and made himself another drink, checked the cash drawer, out of habit, then gave the tip jar a glance. The girls would have a nice tip day, if the heat kept up. Jack eased back onto his 'owner's stool' and sipped his drink.

"Are Baptists welcome in this establishment?" Otis Forbes asked, as he sidled up to the bar and took the stool next to Jack.

"Sure, if they are of the Southern variety, and at least a hundred miles away from their congregation," Jack replied.

Jack set his drink down, swung around, and grinned. Otis was dressed in a tropical worsted white suit, white shoes, white shirt with a black string tie, and a white panama straw-hat.

"Hey, there, Boss Hog."

"Pardon, Jack?"

"Nothing, Otis, I was just thinking out loud. What brings you out in this heat?"

"How about offering me a drink first? By God, it's a hot one," Otis said, as he fanned himself with his hat and pulled at his collar.

Jack yelled out, "Lamont, shoot Mr. Forbes a Southern Comfort over ice."

Lamont put a napkin down, placed the drink on it, and put a bowl of salted nuts in front of Otis. "Anything else, Mr. Forbes?"

"No, Lamont, this should do me, until I get back to the office," he answered with a polite smile reserved for the help.

Otis took a healthy gulp. "By God, that's refreshing…now, to business, Jack. I have a few papers, I need for you to sign, old boy. Should only take a minute," he said, as he pulled a sheaf of papers out of his jacket pocket.

"Let's start with Ms. Duvalier, shall we…?"

"Start what? She's not here, Otis. She's still up in Miami with Bill Price and won't be back for another couple of weeks," Jack said, puzzled.

"No matter, you can sign as her Power of Attorney…"

"Sign what? I don't have her power of attorney…"

"Well, actually, you do. Her authorizing signature is just a formality we can do later, so just shut up, and let me explain." Otis was all business, as he shuffled the papers around into several stacks.

"Sign here…here…and initial here."

Jack signed in the spaces indicated. "What have I just signed, Otis?"

"Starting at the first of next month, Ms. Duvalier will receive twenty thousand dollars, and the first of every month going forward, a like amount. These monies are distributions out of a trust fund set up by her mother, Renee Duvalier before Coco was born…"

"Trust fund…before she was born…what are you talking about"

Otis exhaled loudly, as he turned slowly, and stared into Jack's eyes. "Don't be obtuse, Jack."

Jack looked, puzzled for a moment, then realization sunk in. "Why, you old thief…"

"Tut tut, old boy, loose lips and all that rot," Otis said, as he went back to his papers. "At some point, we'll need Ms. Duvalier to come into the office and grant the bank authority to handle her financial affairs between herself and the Banc de Brasilia in Rio de Janeiro.

Jack sat in wonder, at what he was hearing. This was the best news he had heard in weeks. "Otis, is this clean? She won't get into any trouble, will she...?"

"By God, man, how dare you insinuate that the Forbes Group would be involved in anything illegal? The full faith and credit of the Forbes Financial Institution stands behind all of its international dealings," Otis said, in mock indignation.

"I feel much better knowing that, Mr. Forbes."

"Then let's continue, on another matter, concerning the Marsh Salvage Operation's claim against Senor Juan Perdido and the Perdido Salvage Company of Vera Cruz de Mexico. You will be happy to know that they have settled your claim of ownership to the wreck of the MS Chula Vista and its cargo of nickel ore..." Correct Senor with the thingy ^

"Perdido Salvage...Vera Cruz...MS Chula Vista?" Jack recited. ???

"Indeed."

"Indeed?"

"Undeniably."

"How much did I settle for?'

"Two and a half million American dollars."

"Truly?"

"Indeed."

The End

Made in the USA
San Bernardino, CA
12 August 2019